MARIE
CURIUS
GIRL GENIUS

First American Edition 2022
Kane Miller, A Division of EDC Publishing

First published in Great Britain in 2020 by The Watts Publishing Group
Text copyright © Orchard Books, 2020
Illustrations copyright © Orchard Books, 2020
The moral rights of the author and illustrator have been waived.
All characters and events in this publication, other than those clearly
in the public domain, are fictitious and any resemblance to real persons,
living or dead, is purely coincidental.

For information contact:
Kane Miller, A Division of EDC Publishing
5402 S 122nd E Ave, Tulsa, OK 74146
www.kanemiller.com
www.myubam.com

Library of Congress Control Number: 2021930344
Printed and bound in the United States of America
1 2 3 4 5 6 7 8 9 10
ISBN: 978-1-68464-352-3

MARIE CURIOUS
GIRL GENIUS

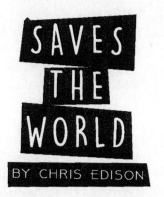

SAVES THE WORLD

BY CHRIS EDISON

Kane Miller
A DIVISION OF EDC PUBLISHING

With thanks to Inclusive Minds for connecting
us with their Inclusion Ambassador network,
and in particular to Emma Zipfel for their input.

Contents

Chapter One

As soon as she got home from school, Marie Trelawney shrugged off her blazer, hung it up carefully and pulled on a white lab coat. She headed across the backyard of her terraced house toward a shed with KEEP OUT written in luminous paint on the door. With her notebook and a package of cookies under her arm, she unlocked the door and let herself into her favorite place in the whole world – her Inventing Shed.

At twelve, Marie was taller than most and looked out onto the world with wide, inquisitive eyes. An almost invisible dusting of freckles lay across the bridge of her

nose. Her neat, sable braids hung down to her shoulders. Instead of jewelry she wore three silicone wristbands: one read M.S. AWARENESS, another YOUNG CARERS, and the third had once read OUR PRINCESS in silver letters but the writing had rubbed off long ago.

Unlike most sheds, there were no lawn mowers, rusty wheelbarrows or bikes gathering cobwebs inside. A throw rug covered the floorboards, and strings of fairy lights hung down from the ceiling, lighting the room in shifting rainbow colors. The walls were covered in posters, most of which Marie had made herself. Up at the top was a cartoon of Katherine Johnson, the genius who calculated how the first NASA spaceflight could orbit the earth. Farther down there were photographs of Marie's other favorite female scientists, a framed certificate for winning the Huxley School Science Fair and a picture of a pug wearing a lab coat and goggles.

Marie had known she wanted to be an inventor since she was little. Back then, she'd driven her mother crazy by taking household items apart. Like the time when she'd rewired the toaster and almost burned the house down, just so she could find out how it worked. Her mum had nicknamed her Marie Curious after the French scientist and her curiosity about all things mechanical had only grown stronger over the years. The shelves inside the Inventing Shed were lined with her gadgets and contraptions.

Marie sat down in the enormous, lumpy armchair she'd been given when her neighbor had moved and set her notebook on the workbench. It was a grubby, glorious thing filled with doodles and designs and covered in stains. There were tea stains, oil stains, soup stains and one or two cat paw prints.

"Izzy!" called Marie, helping herself to a cookie.

A scrappy cat appeared at the half-open window, yawned lazily and squeezed in. Izzy, named after the famous engineer Isambard Kingdom Brunel, paraded back and forth on the workbench, trampling on the pages of Marie's open notebook.

Marie stroked her cat's soft back, enjoying the engine-like rumble of his purr. Apart from her parents, Marie loved nothing more in all the world than her pet cat.

As Izzy batted his head against her hand, Marie grinned and said, "You want to play, don't you?" She reached for a remote control unit and pressed a button on it.

Out from under her workbench shot a robotic mouse with a big dent in his back and one glowing red eye.

"Hi, Ro-DENT!" Marie chuckled. "Feel like giving Izzy some exercise?"

Izzy's pupils grew large. He wiggled his haunches and

pounced. Marie laughed and made Ro-DENT dart away from him.

Marie was very fond of the slightly bashed-up robot mouse she'd invented. Not only could he whizz around on powered wheels, he had magnetic paws so he could scurry up metal surfaces like the fridge, and his eye had a laser pointer built in so he could drive Izzy wild chasing the red dot.

Marie raced Ro-DENT back and forth across the rug, making Izzy perform sudden U-turns and nearly sending him careering into the wall. Then, without warning, Izzy stopped in his tracks and stood there with his ears twitching.

"What's wrong, Iz?" Marie asked. "What can you hear?"

A moment later she heard it herself. A strange high-pitched whine was coming from outside – from above.

It reminded Marie of the sound her mum's electric wheelchair made when it got jammed on the edge of a curb.

She ran out into the yard and looked up. Her eyes went even wider than Izzy's had.

Hovering high over her head was a chunky white delivery drone with four huge rotors the size of trash can lids. It was carrying a parcel.

It won't be for us, Marie thought.

But the drone was already descending. A robotic-sounding voice announced, "Delivery in progress. Please stand back."

The drone touched down lightly on the grass. Marie felt like she was having an alien encounter.

"Mum!" she yelled. "Come and look at this!"

The drone released its package. Then it shot up into the air, much faster than it had landed. Marie shaded

her eyes and watched it whizz over the North London rooftops until it was gone.

She spotted the "V" logo on the box's side. VanceCorp! Only the biggest tech company in the entire world. Something techy must be in this box. A new phone, or even a new tablet.

"Mum!" she called again. "You've got a parcel!"

But as she bent down to pick the box up, she saw who it was addressed to. Not her mum, Dina Trelawney, but her. Marie Trelawney.

"Whoa. *I've* got a parcel?"

Marie was puzzled – her birthday wasn't for another few months. She quickly ripped the silver tape off and opened the box. The inside was packed full of little V-shaped wood-chip pieces. Izzy would have a mad time with those later. Marie shoved her hands into them and fished around like it was a grab bag.

One hand came up holding a glossy pamphlet with the VanceCorp logo on the front. Her other hand found a heavy black cube covered with some smooth, rubbery substance. Silicone, Marie guessed. She tossed the pamphlet aside and turned the cube around in her hands, gazing at it in speechless wonder. What was it?

A battery? A doorstop?

Marie's mum finally appeared at the patio door, wearing her favorite hat. She quickly slid the glass door open before Marie could run up and do it first, and drove her wheelchair out onto their little patio. "Is it the Amazon man?" she called uncertainly.

Marie sprinted up the steps and joined her at the patio table. "No, a drone dropped it off. It's from VanceCorp. Did you order it?"

"Me? No, I'm saving up for a booster to make this thing go faster," she said, patting her wheelchair affectionately.

As she placed the box on the table, Marie's mind suddenly flashed to a memory of a sunny summer morning, when her dad would cook scrambled eggs and bacon for breakfast and they'd all eat around the table. They hadn't done that in ages, not since he'd gotten a job on an oil rig in the North Sea. Marie and her mum missed him dearly, but taking the job had meant that they had enough money for Mum to quit her job when she had gotten sick, and it helped pay for a nurse to come and help her when she was having a bad day.

Marie turned the cube over in her hands and wondered what it was for. One of the faces had the fancy VanceCorp "V" logo, but the other sides were blank.

"How do you turn it on?" she wondered.

"Aren't there any instructions with it?" her mum teased.

Marie remembered the pamphlet, which she hadn't

even opened. "You know I don't read instructions," she said. "That's like cheating."

She set the cube down and gave it a hard stare.

Izzy bounded up onto the table, still wild-eyed and bushy-tailed from chasing Ro-DENT earlier. He flattened his ears and swatted at the cube, trying to knock it off the table.

"Oh no no no, you big lump. This isn't a toy." Marie tried to pick him up but he squirmed and struggled. One of his paws pressed down on the "V."

Click. The cube made a deep purring noise.

Izzy bristled and launched himself out of Marie's arms. He bounded across the yard, scrambled up a tree and glared balefully down from a branch.

"It's opening!" yelled Marie's mum.

Where the "V" had been, there was now a little hole. Marie leaned closer for a better look.

A cone of blue light suddenly sprang up from the cube, and Marie and her mother gasped in shock. It faded away to reveal a hologram of a doll-sized white man standing in front of them. He wore a gleaming metallic jumpsuit and dark glasses, like an astronaut, and his silver hair was swept back from his suntanned face. His boots were chunky and had blue rocket jets burning from the heels.

Izzy hissed.

Marie's mouth fell open. "That's ... that's ... Sterling Vance! The head of VanceCorp!"

"Hey there," said Sterling Vance, and bowed.

"It is and all!" exclaimed Marie's mum.

"I have a special message for Marie," Vance said.

Marie let out a little squeak. This was like getting a text from Beyoncé or a birthday card from Bill Gates. Everyone Marie knew either had a Vance phone or

wanted one. The teachers at her school used Vance laptops. You couldn't watch TV without that familiar "You can't say advancement without saying Vance!" commercial coming on.

Vance grinned, showing perfect teeth. "Marie, it's my pleasure to tell you that your project on 'Cleaning Up Our Cities with Robots' has won you a place at Vance Camp!"

Marie couldn't even speak. Her mother put her hands to her cheeks. "Oh my days."

"Now, as if you didn't know this already," Vance went on, "Vance Camp is the world's most famous summer camp for young scientists! I only take the best, so just thirty kids are selected each year. We've got classes, workshops, all kinds of fun, and of course, the all-important secret contest. So congratulations, champ! You've already proven you're no loser. But have you

got what it takes to really win big? I guess we'll find out soon," he said cheerfully, and winked. "In the meantime, meet your new friends. Also known as the competition. *Adios!*"

The projection of Sterling Vance vanished. In his place appeared a slowly rotating carousel of portraits. Marie and her mum leaned in to look at them. Each one had a name underneath in glowing text.

"There I am!" Marie yelled excitedly as the image of her own face moved by.

"Look at them all," her mother said in awe. "Check this boy out! Jacques Belmont. Nice cheekbones. And this one, Melissa van Chamonix. She looks posh! And what about him? Zachary G. Boomer. Sounds like an astronaut!"

Marie fell silent as she watched the faces go by. The hugeness of what was happening began to sink in.

She was going to the United States of America, to an exclusive science camp. She'd be away from home – away from Mum! – for the first time ever.

So many strangers. So many unknown faces. But they all looked young and bright. Surely some of them would be her friends ... wouldn't they?

Chapter Two

Marie couldn't sit still.

It had been a restless eleven-hour flight from London Heathrow to Los Angeles International. Now that she was nearly at her destination, nerves had kicked in too.

She'd worn her softest jeans and her favorite NASA T-shirt on the flight, but even so, she couldn't get comfy. She'd tied her long, smooth braids up with her lucky hair band and slipped on her smart sunglasses. They weren't like normal glasses; the lenses were hexagonal and the glass changed color

every time you looked at them. They had baffled the security guard at Heathrow when she sent them through the X-ray scanner. "These have a microchip in them," he'd said, astonished. "But how did you make one so small?"

"It's easy once you know how," Marie replied, taking the glasses from the stunned guard and skipping off to her gate.

Skreee! Marie flinched as a high-pitched squeal jarred her nerves. The flight attendant's cart had a squeaky wheel and nobody was doing anything about it.

To pass the time, Marie unfolded the glossy VanceCorp brochure and smoothed it out over her tray table. The famous Vance Pyramid gleamed on the page, a miracle of steel and glass surrounded by green lawns and arching fountains. Her heart jittered.

In only a few hours, she'd be inside that incredible building.

As Marie leafed through the brochure, she reflected on how much she still didn't know about Vance Camp. The thought made her even more nervous and fidgety. It wasn't that there was anything sinister about the company. VanceCorp had a worldwide reputation for quality, after all. The company gave oodles of money to charity, and funded projects like science fairs and summer camps. It was just that nobody who had ever been to Vance Camp was allowed to talk about it afterward. They even made you sign a special form.

"It makes sense," Marie had told her suspicious mum. "They're developing all sorts of cool, top secret projects. They don't want us to go and talk to the competition, do they?"

The next page showed the dormitories. They looked

luxurious, with enormous bathrooms and wall-sized TVs, but Marie swallowed hard. This was a big jump for someone who'd never been away from home for any length of time.

Skreee! went the wheel on the refreshments cart again, right next to her. Marie yelped aloud, then breathed out and rolled her eyes. "So smooth," she muttered.

"Um ... excuse me, miss?" The flight attendant tapped her gently on the shoulder. "Would you like anything?"

Marie glanced at the drinks and snacks, then down at the squeaky wheel. "Yes. I'd like to fix your cart, please."

The flight attendant opened his mouth to speak, but before he could get a word out, Marie went into action. She lunged down, caught the edge of the cart and with

all her strength, lifted it up just enough to tug the wheel out of its socket.

Instantly, without even putting her glasses into magnify mode, she saw what was wrong. A rubber band had gotten wound around the axle. Marie fished in her pocket for a bobby pin, found one, and used it to lever the band out. A quick test spin, and now the wheel whizzed around easily.

She reached down, clicked it back into place then leaned back and let out a long, happy sigh. "Thanks!"

The flight attendant blinked. "I ... uh ... you're welcome, I guess?" He moved on to the next passenger. The cart trundled past, nice and quiet now.

Marie loved the feeling of having fixed something, even if it was only a squeaky wheel. It was almost as sweet as the feeling she got when she'd taken a new invention from design to reality. Her glasses were her

best invention so far. They didn't just look fabulous, they held hidden secrets, too.

She checked that her laptop was logged in to the plane's onboard Wi-Fi and connected it to her glasses via Bluetooth. A quick flick of the switch on the frame changed the glasses from everyday mode to digital mode. She settled back in her seat to watch her favorite video feed!

Her glasses showed her a cat's-eye view of her own backyard in London. The video stream was a little juddery, but Marie was glad to get any kind of connection up here among the clouds. "Hi, Izzy," she whispered and grinned.

The night before, Marie had mounted a VanceVision webcam to Izzy's collar. Now she'd be able to lie in bed at night and keep him company on his prowls, seeing what he saw.

"Go check on Mum," Marie urged.

As if he'd heard her from hundreds of miles away, Izzy bounded across the lawn. He dived through his cat flap and into the house. He wandered between chair legs, scampered into the living room and hopped up into Marie's mum's lap.

Marie's heart ached as Izzy looked up into her mum's smiling face. She thought back to the promise she'd made on the day the drone had arrived, three months ago.

"You just wait, Mum. I'll make the most of Vance Camp – make loads of high-up connections, become an engineer, earn millions, buy us a new smart home, and program the whole place to make your life easier!"

"And what about Izzy?" her mum had teased.

"I'll make him a heated cat bed. And then I'll

help find a cure for ..." She'd gestured at her mum's wheelchair.

Her mum had shaken her head then. "Oh, Marie. You can't fix everything, you know."

"I can learn. And I will. From the best."

"You are *twelve*! You need to make friends. Have fun. Don't grow up too fast, love."

A heavy clunk jerked Marie back to reality. The plane's landing gear! She pushed the glasses up onto the top of her head. Through the window she could see land below. The thought of being in a new country sent fresh thrills through her.

The flight attendant was back. "Ready for landing, miss?"

Marie quickly fastened her seat belt. "I am now."

"Not quite," said the flight attendant, putting her tray table up.

"Sorry," said Marie. "First time flying by myself."

"Don't sweat it. And hey. This is for fixing my cart before." He pressed a bar of chocolate into her hand, winked, and left.

Marie stared in wonder at the bar, with its unfamiliar wrapper. American chocolate. Just like the whole trip, she had no idea what to expect.

But, she thought as she excitedly began to unwrap it, *there's only one way to find out ...*

I'm really here, Marie thought. She was sitting in the back seat of an air-conditioned SUV looking out of the window at Los Angeles. *Those palm trees aren't on TV. They're real. Should I pinch myself? Do people actually do that?*

To her left was a boy with his hair shaved into a crisp fade. He seemed just as excited as her. The blond white girl on Marie's right stared at her tablet and scrolled through web pages.

"You all OK back there?" called Becca from the front seat. Becca was a tall, bright-eyed VanceCorp engineer and Marie had liked her immediately. When Becca had explained that she'd be their camp counselor, half of Marie's worries had vanished on the spot. Now they were on their way to Vance Camp, the last group of kids to arrive.

"Loving it!" Marie called back.

"Fantastique," said the boy, giving a thumbs-up.

His French accent rang a bell in Marie's memory. She glanced at his face, trying to look casual. What was it her mum had said? Nice cheekbones ...

"Jacques Belmont?" she guessed.

He turned to her and grinned, showing the metal braces on his teeth. "And you're Marie," he said. "Go, team Europe!" He offered her a fist bump. She accepted.

Marie felt happily caught up in the moment. She turned and held her own fist out to the blond girl.

Nothing happened. The girl didn't even look up.

"Hi," Marie prompted. "Who are you?"

"Ingrid De Meyer," the girl said, with about as much warmth and feeling as a roll of aluminum foil.

"Where are you from?" Marie asked.

"Nunnia."

Marie frowned. She'd never heard of it. "Nunnia?"

"Nunnia business." Ingrid glanced at Marie from under her thick platinum-blond bangs. "I'm not here to make friends. Didn't you get Vance's message in your cube? You're the competition."

Marie took the hint and turned away. Jacques

caught her eye and they both shrugged.

The rest of the journey passed in an awkward silence, but luckily it wasn't very long. Tires soon crunched on gravel and they came to a stop. "Welcome to the VanceCorp campus," Becca called. "This is where the magic happens!"

Marie climbed out into the sunshine. A cool breeze ruffled her hair. There, filling her view, was the Vance Pyramid. The size of it took her breath away. Floor after glass-fronted floor reached up to the sky, all filled with laboratories, design studios and computer centers.

"It's beautiful," she breathed.

She glanced from the pyramid to the smaller buildings that surrounded it like little stooping attendants, and tried to take it all in. All around the campus, people were hurrying from one place to

another, riding on moving walkways or rising up in gravity-defying elevators.

To Marie's surprise, the sky was full of swooping, gliding white shapes. Were they seagulls, perhaps? The VanceCorp headquarters was right on the coast, after all. Maybe the people who worked here liked to feed them.

A bird zoomed toward her. As it flew closer, she realized it wasn't a bird at all. It was a drone, just like the one that had delivered her package.

"Say hello to the Robutler," said Becca. "Better get used to these guys. They're robot butlers, and they do pretty much all the work around here."

The Robutler dropped down, hovered in front of Marie and scanned her with its single red eye. "Good morning, Miss Trelawney. May I take your luggage?"

Marie gave the Robutler her bag. It reached out

to take her precious notebook, too, but she tucked it under her arm and held it there tightly. "It's OK. I'll keep this on me."

Marie watched openmouthed as the Robutler whisked her suitcase away through the air. Then Becca led her through to join the other campers, and Marie became part of a lively, excited, jostling crowd of kids. Faces she vaguely recognized from the cube's display surrounded her.

Becca and several other jumpsuited engineers shepherded the campers through the pyramid's vast entrance hall, past display cases and into the dark empty space of an auditorium.

Marie looked around for Jacques and Ingrid, but they seemed to have melted into the crowd. She sat down in a random seat. Her palms were damp.

A girl with silky brown hair and cool pink

headphones around her neck sat next to her. Marie smiled at her, and to her relief, the girl smiled back.

"Hi. I'm Marie Trelawney," said Marie.

"Gabriella Diaz," the girl said, "but you can call me Gabby. All my friends do."

Marie took a breath, eager to bombard Gabby with questions, but she never got the chance. The overhead lights dimmed to darkness and voices across the auditorium quieted to whispers.

A brilliant spotlight shone down from above. A man in a silvery blue suit strolled out of the darkness and into the beam's glare. Gabby and Marie recognized him immediately.

"Sterling Vance!" Marie whispered. "In the flesh!"

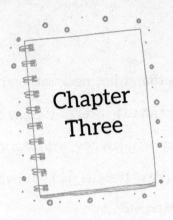

Chapter Three

Sterling Vance walked to the center of the stage and the spotlight tracked across to follow him. Tiny lights chased up and down the seams of his suit.

He raised his hands.

Marie held her breath. The entire auditorium fell silent. Everyone waited to hear what the great inventor would say.

"Some people say science is boring," Vance said. "They're wrong. Science is power. Science is knowledge. Science lets me do this."

He flung his hand out, blasting a power chord on an

electric guitar that suddenly appeared from nowhere. The stage exploded with sound, color and light.

Behind Vance, a colossal robot skull rose up from the floor. Its eyes were rotating planets made of flame, its teeth glittering jewels that projected rainbow beams of light out over the crowd. The skull opened its jaws, and a stampede of metal unicorns came thundering out. They galloped overhead, their manes streaming behind, shooting out sparks like comet trails.

Spaceships roared past next, shattering into glimmering shards as neon tanks fired up at them. Albert Einstein galloped down the center aisle on a saber-toothed tiger, brandishing a foaming test tube and waving.

"Allo, Albert!" cried Jacques, giving him a high five.

All the while, Vance kept up a twiddly solo on his holographic guitar, until with a sudden violent twist he

turned and flung it into the robot skull's gaping mouth. Marie felt her chair vibrate. The skull vanished and a slow, fiery mushroom cloud explosion rose in its place, then faded away to nothing.

A stunned silence followed. Then someone started to clap, and they all joined in, whooping and cheering.

"Muy loco," Gabby whispered.

"So!" boomed Vance. "Now you've seen what science can do in the hands of a company like VanceCorp. But what is science? Maybe it's easier if I just show you."

Behind Vance appeared a giant photograph. It was a faded Polaroid of a boy of about three sitting on the floor, holding what was left of a toy robot. Bits and pieces of the toy lay around him. The boy had a huge, cheeky grin.

The audience laughed.

"Yep, that's me," said Vance. "And that's the moment

when I became a scientist. Hopefully, all of you guys understand. If you don't, then I guess ... maybe you don't belong here after all."

Vance let that comment hang in the air. Marie could definitely identify with the little boy in the picture, who had taken his toy apart, but somehow Vance's challenge made her feel uncomfortable. Someone coughed.

Then Vance grinned again and spread his arms wide. "Welcome, each and every one of you! In honor of my childhood self up there, we've given camp a special theme this year. Robotics!"

"Woo-hoo!" Marie cheered before she could stop herself.

Scattered laughter broke out. Marie cringed into her seat, but then Vance gave her a thumbs-up and she felt better. He reminded her of a wacky game show host.

"We've flown in some of the world's top scientists

for tutorials and workshops," Vance said. "You're here to learn and to have fun, but mainly to compete. So listen up. Whoever designs the most impressive robot, as decided by our panel of judges, wins the grand prize – a yearlong apprenticeship with yours truly! And on top of that, an all-expenses-paid trip to the world's biggest tech fair!"

Gasps of surprise came from all around.

Marie bit her knuckles. An apprenticeship with Vance would mean that she could learn from the best, with the top tech. It might even help her to get into a top university like MIT, to study engineering. Some of the most brilliant brains in science had studied there – astronauts like Buzz Aldrin, architects like I.M. Pei, and of course one of Marie's personal heroines – physicist Shirley Ann Jackson. Winning this robotics competition would be a passport to an exciting career,

the future she'd dreamed of – and the kind of life her mum deserved.

Marie glanced over at Gabby, who had her eyes closed and seemed to be praying. Her heart went out to her. No doubt Gabby was thinking of her own future, too, and maybe even her own mother.

Stop that, Marie thought to herself. *I've got to win.* She remembered what Ingrid had said. *I have to start thinking of the other kids as my competition.*

"Good luck to all of you," Vance said. "Enjoy the camp. Work hard. Chase your dreams. Even if you find you have stars in your eyes, don't worry – because science is what takes us to the stars."

From offstage, a billowing mass of fog rolled across the floor. It drifted out and blanketed the whole stage in a thick layer of mist, pouring over the front edge. Vance's lower body was swallowed up in the clouds.

A look of concentration came over his face. His body began to glide backward through the mist, as if he were floating on the fog. The crowd began to chatter in amazement as waves of fog swept Sterling Vance off the stage.

When the fog had cleared, Becca bounded up onto the stage. "Wow! So, guys, are you impressed yet?"

"YEAH!" roared everyone.

"Cool. Now, a word of warning. Mr. Vance might be able to walk on clouds, but you guys have a long way to go before you reach that level. None of you are going to make a robot good enough to win the competition unless you put in a lot of hard work. And you all want to win, right?"

"YEAH!" everyone roared again.

"That's the spirit. But don't worry – there will be plenty of fun activities, too, like our annual talent show.

OK, scheduling. Tomorrow morning after breakfast you'll all go on a tour of the Vance campus. After lunch, classes will begin. For the rest of today, just relax! Any questions?"

Jacques put his hand up. "Can I get a map? I don't want to go looking for a bathroom and fall into a nuclear reactor."

Becca quieted the laughter. "We've thought of that. On your way out, remember to pick up your V-bands." Seeing blank looks on the campers' faces, she pointed to the gadget on her wrist. "Behold, the V-band. It hasn't been released yet, but believe me, everyone will want one. It's a smart watch, with 3D holographic phone calling, map navigation and body monitoring as standard. And it tells the time, too!"

As the crowd of kids leapt up and ran to collect their V-bands, Becca called, "Whoa! One more thing. You

guys get to be part of the development process. You'll help to beta test the new upgrade to VanceOS before it gets launched globally. So if you think the V-bands are cool now, wait until they're fully upgraded. That's it! Go!"

Marie turned to Gabby. They said nothing for a second. Then, together, they flailed their hands about and went, "Aaaaaah!" before bursting out laughing.

"This place," said Gabby. "The contest. Everything. I am tripping out, chica."

"I know, right? I can't believe they're just giving away those band things!"

Gabby wiggled her V-phone. "Eight hundred dollars and it's already obsolete."

Chatting like old friends, they strolled out of the auditorium and joined the line for V-bands. Marie forgot all about Gabby being the competition.

"You didn't hear this from me," Gabby said slyly, "but the new system update has augmented reality functions built in."

"Seriously?"

"Oh yeah. Want to see how you'll look in violet eye shadow, or with a kitty nose? Just shine your V-band on your face."

"Waaaait a minute. Becca said V-bands haven't been released yet ... "

"True," Gabby said, doing a bad job of looking innocent.

"So how do you know so much, hmm?"

"Wellll, your girl here just happens to be an expert at coding," Gabby said. "And Mr. Vance doesn't lock the back door on his servers as securely as he should."

"You're a hacker!" gasped Marie.

"Don't be scared. I'm what they call 'white hat.' We're

the good guys."

Marie felt thrilled to the bone. Only yesterday she'd been kicking about in her Invention Shed, and now she was hanging out with a cool American hacker!

"Come on, then! What else did you find out?"

"The upgrade is code-named Black Rose," Gabby whispered. "It's so secret they only let a few people work on it at a time. VanceCorps is racing to get it out fast, before any of its competitors bring out something similar."

But Gabby had to stop there, as they'd reached the front of the line. A guy with a ponytail down to his belt smiled at them. "Hi! I'm Jesse. Gonna need to take an iris scan and a fingerprint."

Jesse's fingers moved in a blur as he entered Marie and Gabby's details in the system. "All done. One V-band for you, and one for you."

Marie fastened the strap around her wrist immediately. The second it touched her skin, the screen came to life. "Hello, Marie," said a friendly robotic voice. "You're showing signs of exhaustion. I recommend a glass of water and a nap."

Gabby laid a hand on her arm. "I forgot. You've flown all the way from England, haven't you?"

"I'm not tired," Marie yawned.

"Uh-huh. Right. Sure." Gabby tapped Marie's V-band. "Show route to Marie's dorm."

Marie jumped as her V-band shone a red arrow into the air in front of her.

"S'pose I should probably find out where those Robutlers took my luggage off to," she said, and yawned again.

"Catch you in the morning," grinned Gabby. "Good luck with your roommate!"

Marie had forgotten all about roommates. This was going to be great! They'd stay up till midnight eating candy and junk food, and telling jokes that only other science-y girls would get. She hurried along the hallways and up the elevators, following the hovering red arrow.

Eventually, she found her room. Inside Marie saw an open suitcase sitting on the bed and clothes everywhere.

"Hellooo?" Marie called. "Anyone home?"

"Oh, great," came the sarcastic response.

Marie stepped into the room. Her heart sank. Standing there with her hands on her hips was Ingrid, the steely-eyed girl from the car ride. And judging from the look on her face, Marie's roommate thought the entire room belonged to her ...

Chapter Four

"Urrrrgh," Marie groaned into her pillow. It was time to get up, but she didn't want to move. She felt like she'd slept for about a day, and it still hadn't been enough.

At least the bed was comfortable. It was set into the wall, meaning you were boxed in on all but one side. Marie had discovered that the open side could be closed off, too, giving you complete privacy. *How do I open it?* she wondered, trying to remember where the button was.

"Open bed," she said, just to see what would happen.

The panel slid upward and Californian sunshine

poured in.

Marie lifted her head, winced, and glanced around warily. Ingrid's things were still all over the room and her bed was a mess, but there was no sign of her. Good. The sullen girl must already have left for the day.

"Fine by me," Marie muttered.

She tried to remember what had happened the night before. She'd barely said two words to Ingrid before climbing into bed and passing out. In fact, she hadn't even had a good look around the room.

Marie shuffled backward up the bed and propped herself up, noticing for the first time that there were screens set into the surfaces above and beside the bed. The room itself was huge, bigger than the entire ground floor of her house in London. In one corner was an exercise machine that Ingrid had draped her clothes over. Nearby was one of those huge fridges with the

double doors and a drink dispenser in the front. There were two sumptuously soft beanbag chairs in front of a big curved screen that Marie guessed was an expensive gaming console of some sort.

"Tea, please," she said aloud, wondering if it would work. Across the room, the drink dispenser gurgled and hissed. Marie swung her legs over the edge of the bed, stretched and went to fetch the tea.

I'd better get Mum's tea too, she thought out of habit, then felt a pang. Mum was thousands of miles away.

"I am such a zombie," she said to herself. "Why am I so tired?"

Out of nowhere, a friendly voice replied, "Because you are suffering from jet lag."

Marie sat down heavily on the bed. "Hello?" she whispered.

"Hello, Marie," the voice replied.

"Ah, no disrespect, but ... who is this?"

"My name is Jenny. I am the Vance Interface System."

Marie sighed in relief, suddenly recognizing the voice from her V-band. Of course. "Run me through the basics, please," she instructed Jenny.

For the next ten minutes, Marie learned all about voice controls, and when she was done she knew everything from how to order a midnight delivery of candy bars to how to activate the emergency fire escape.

"I have learned your preferences. Customizing room now," said Jenny.

Marie sat in amazement as the room changed around her. Her capsule bed shifted to a peaceful shade of blue. A gentle sound of waves came through the speakers and the air filled with her favorite smell – freshly cut grass. Finally, little laser projectors created twinkles on the walls, reminding Marie of the fairy lights back in her

Inventing Shed.

"Oh, wow! I love it. Thanks!"

Marie lay back and enjoyed her new room for a moment. The homesickness hadn't gone away, though. She wished she could talk to her mum, and with a start she realized she could.

"Call Dina Trelawney," Marie told her V-band.

It took only seconds for the call to connect. Her mum's concerned face appeared on the screen by Marie's bed.

"You're still in bed!" Mum shouted. "It's four in the afternoon!"

Marie burst out laughing. "It's morning here in California, Mum. We're eight hours behind you, remember?"

She launched into a breathless description of her trip so far. When she got to the part about Ingrid, her mum told her not to worry. "She's acting that way because

she's shy," she said. "Don't let her get to you."

Marie noticed a splash of spilled cornflakes on the floor behind her mum. "What's that?"

"Nothing."

Marie's stomach clenched. "Did you drop your breakfast?"

"Marie! It was just a little accident, you hear me? And Kate's here every day to help with the house and things. She'll deal with it. You have got to start having fun and not stress yourself over me!"

"I'll try," Marie said, not feeling very certain.

"Hello, Marie," Jenny interrupted. "This is a courtesy announcement. You have fifteen minutes left before breakfast ends. You are low on nutrients. Please eat a healthy breakfast today."

Marie's mum's mouth formed an O. "Listen. She's got a new robot mum already!"

"Got to go, Mum! Love you. I'll call again soon."

Marie quickly finished her tea and pulled her clothes on. Twelve minutes left. She bounded over to the door, which slid open automatically.

She stopped in her tracks and blinked. Sterling Vance was standing outside the door, as if he'd been about to knock. He was wearing a plain gray business suit. Marie stared. He looked so normal. Where had the zany showman from yesterday gone?

"Can we talk?" he said. He even sounded different. More like a bank manager than a game show host.

Marie struggled to get words out. "Um. Sure. I mean, yes?"

"Cool. Listen up, I've only got a few seconds. What I've got to tell you is top secret, and you mustn't tell anyone else. Not a soul. Got it?"

"Got it," Marie said.

Vance peered at her over the top of his glasses. "There is a spy at Vance Camp. A rival company must have sent them – maybe Hayes-Belker, or maybe Sorensen. But I'm sure of one thing. There is a spy in our midst."

"You mean it's one of us campers?" Marie gasped.

"That's why I need you on my side, kid."

"What should I do?"

"Don't trust anyone. Be on the alert for people snooping around, acting suspicious. If you get any leads, let me know. Now hurry along. We mustn't be seen together."

Marie started off down the corridor, but suddenly realized she didn't know how to contact Vance directly. She turned around.

There was nobody there. Vance was gone, like a ghost.

"Weird." Marie shuddered.

She hurried on toward the dining hall, pushing past employees sipping their morning coffees. She couldn't stop thinking about what Vance had told her. On the way into breakfast, she nearly crashed into Ingrid who was leaving.

"You finally got out of bed, I see," Ingrid sniffed.

"Yeah, thanks for waking me up in time for breakfast, roomie," Marie snapped back. She skirted around Ingrid and went into the dining hall.

As she waited in the line, she kept mulling over the strange conversation she'd had with Sterling Vance. *Why did he pick ME to tell?* she wondered.

Maybe he suspected that the spy was Ingrid! That would certainly explain why her roommate was trying to keep her at a distance. *I don't have any proof*, thought Marie, remembering what her mother had said about Ingrid just being shy.

The delicious smell of hot food was making her hungry. Transparent shelves with little doors held hash browns, biscuits, waffles, pancakes, syrup, cereal and heaps of bacon. She looked up to see a robot chef flipping a pancake and catching it perfectly.

"Just scan your V-band over whatever you want," another camper told Marie, demonstrating with his own band and helping himself to a plate of pancakes.

Marie moved to the end where the bowls of sugary choco-flakes with marshmallows were waiting. When she waved her V-band over them, it flashed red and buzzed. "Health alert!" it said. "The dish you have selected is not nutritionally balanced!"

"Not bothered," Marie said, grabbing two bowlfuls.

The dining hall was crowded, and Marie wasn't sure where she ought to sit. Then she saw Gabby and Jacques waving to her from across the room. Feeling relieved,

she went to sit with them.

"Just in time!" Jacques shuffled up a space so Marie could sit opposite Gabby. A brown-eyed girl in a hijab was sitting next to her and smiled at Marie.

"Marie, this is Elisha Amin," Gabby said. "She's from India."

Marie was about to hold out her hand, but Elisha smiled again and put her right hand over her heart. "Salaam," she said softly, bowing slightly. Marie did the same.

"So what about that intro we got yesterday, huh?" Gabby said. "Wasn't that intense?"

"Monsieur Vance is amazing!" Jacques said. "The things they let us see – you know how many of his inventions these are?" He held up his thumb and forefinger with a tiny gap between them. "This many. Under this building, there are tunnels." (He pronounced

it *toon-ells*, and Marie tried not to laugh.) "They go deep under the ground. He has whole teams, making secret inventions."

"Like what?" Marie asked, wide-eyed.

"Mole machines. Giant laser cannons. Underground hover trains. Even his own private fleet of soucoupes volantes!"

"Sou-whats?" Gabby asked, puzzled.

"Flying saucers," Jacques translated.

Marie didn't want to leave Elisha out of the conversation. "What did you think of Vance's performance, Elisha?" she asked.

Elisha looked at Marie from under long eyelashes. "Loud," she said.

Marie shoveled cereal into her mouth while Jacques kept on about Vance's secret inventions. "I can't believe I'm actually here," he said. "What do you think other

tech companies would do to get inside this building, with all of its secrets? How much do you think they would pay?" He winked at Marie.

Marie almost choked on her cereal. Did he know? Was Jacques the spy?

"Well, I'm ready for the robot-building contest," Gabby said. "Bring it on."

"You have an idea already?" Jacques said. "What is it?"

"Nice try!" Gabby snorted. "You think I'm gonna share?"

"How about you, Marie?" Jacques grinned.

"I, uh, haven't had time to think about it," Marie said. All of a sudden she felt queasy, and not just because she'd wolfed down two bowls of cereal. What was she going to design?

"It's fine." Jacques shrugged, pretending to be hurt. "I

get it. I'm the competition. Don't tell me."

Gabby slurped her drink through a purple straw, and her V-band beeped an alert which she ignored. "No offense, but the real competition is that Dutch girl, Ingrid. You know she's last year's runner-up? Seems she was so set on winning, she managed to get into Vance Camp twice. Nobody's ever done that before."

"Oh," Marie said, suddenly feeling like she understood Ingrid a lot better. Coming second must have stung her badly.

Gabby's V-band beeped again. Checking it, she frowned and stood up. "Breakfast time's over, guys. I just got a text from Becca. It's time for the tour to start!"

Chapter Five

Marie, Gabby, Elisha and Jacques hurried through the bustling corridors. Marie glanced into the offices and conference rooms they passed, wondering if the people who worked here ever got used to it. She ached to have a good look around the offices, but there wasn't time. *One day*, she said to herself, *that could be me working here.*

"Meeting point is in the atrium, under the atom sculpture," Gabby said.

"I see it!" Marie yelled.

Down in the open area at the bottom of the pyramid was a space like a town square, with coffee kiosks

and benches. Towering over it all was a shiny metal sculpture of an atom. The electrons slowly orbited around the nucleus, hovering in the air somehow. Marie wondered if it was done with magnets. However much it might look like magic, VanceCorp was all about science.

Becca waved up at them. "You're just in time! Grab a board and get ready to glide."

The "boards" turned out to be flat white things about the size of a tea tray, with two places to put your feet, a long strut in the middle and handlebars like a scooter. Marie climbed onto hers. With a soft beep and a slight vibration, the board came to life. The handles lit up and Marie felt herself rise a few centimeters into the air.

"Whoa!" she cried, nearly losing her balance.

"Don't worry, you won't fall off," Becca said.

Once all thirty of the camp kids had climbed onto their hoverboards, Becca tapped her V-band. "I'm setting

you all to autopilot. No going off on joyrides just yet."

"Awww," pouted Jacques.

"Don't worry, there'll be plenty of time to goof around with the boards afterward. Ready? Let's go!"

Marie held on tight as her board began to move. With Becca at the head of the group, they all moved into a wedge formation, like flying geese. The staff in the atrium clapped and cheered for the camp kids as they swept past and out of the main pyramid building. Marie's board picked up speed, the wind ruffled her hair, and she felt like the queen of the world.

Becca nimbly flipped her board so she was facing the group, but still moving forward. "At Vance, we do three things. Work hard, play hard and relax. I'm going to show you the last two first."

The first stopping point was the swimming pool. Marie couldn't believe it when her hoverboard reached

the edge of the pool and kept going, levitating above the water's surface.

"Nothing clears the mind after a hard day's coding like a go on the waterslide," explained Becca.

"Cool!" said a blond girl with an Australian accent, her eyes the exact same shade of blue as the sparkling water.

Next, Becca showed them flotation tanks with virtual reality headsets. "When you really need to get away from the crowds," said Becca, "you can drift among the stars, or dive into the depths of the sea."

The tour party moved on to the squash courts, where you could play against a Robutler. Then came the Zen Garden, which offered a choice of traditional stone stacking and sand arranging – strictly no tech anywhere nearby.

Everywhere they went, Marie saw robots doing

jobs. One of them was mowing the lawn, while another washed windows with sponge-tipped arms and another trimmed the hedges. *This is like living in the future*, Marie thought in wonder.

Eventually they pulled up outside a domed building. Through the glass door, Marie could make out colorful soft furniture like something from a children's play center.

"And now," Becca said, "for my favorite facility. Some days you get stressed, even working at an awesome company like this. You know what we do when we really need to unwind?"

She let them in and opened a door. Into the room came ...

"Puppies!" Marie squealed.

The whole group went crazy as puppies came to greet them, wagging their tails and hopping up onto

the campers' laps. Marie and the Australian girl found they were sitting on opposite sides of an adorable little Golden Retriever puppy.

Becca said, "It's scientifically proven that playing with puppies lowers stress levels. Go ahead and pet them. But be gentle."

"Becca?" said Marie. "You do look after these little guys properly, right? I mean ... they don't stay puppies forever."

"Don't worry," Becca said, smiling. "They all get taken to loving homes. Every single one of them."

The Australian girl leaned over and whispered, "Good on ya, mate. I was going to ask the same thing. I'm Sophie. I love animals too. Do you have a dog back home?"

"Marie. And I'm more of a cat person, usually."

Sophie was wearing a denim jacket covered in badges

with rainbows and other symbols, and Marie instantly recognized one she owned herself. "You went on a Climate March too?"

"Did I ever! Talked half the school into coming with me!" Sophie laughed. "Reckon I would have gotten expelled if my grades weren't so high."

Marie spent the rest of the puppy-petting session chatting to Sophie, who didn't seem to have a social filter. She just said exactly what she thought. It was a bit startling, but refreshing too. As they stroked the puppies, she and Sophie discussed the talent show.

"I've got a great idea for a funny magic act," said Sophie, grinning. "Are you in?"

"Sure," said Marie. "Sounds fun." She couldn't remember ever having made a friend so quickly.

When their puppy session was over, Becca led them out to a square of gray asphalt. "And now for the work

part of the tour," she announced. "First stop, research and development – R&D for short. This is where we try out our new inventions."

"Yes!" Marie punched the air. This was what she'd been waiting for.

"But this just looks like a parking lot," said Gabby.

Becca grinned. "Open sesame!" She tapped a code into her V-band. The assembled kids gasped as the ground beneath them began to move. Slowly, two great sliding doors rumbled back, revealing a set of hidden laboratories beneath. It was like taking the roof off a dollhouse. The kids were left on the edge, peering down at the white-coated workers.

"We keep the laboratories underground for security and safety reasons," Becca said. "That way we can seal off whole sections if there are any, let's say, mishaps."

The hoverboards zoomed down through the air

and landed next to the workbenches. For the next few hours, Marie was in paradise. First, the Vance technicians showed her how to use a virtual reality design suite. She created an entire model glider from scratch, selecting her materials and shaping them. It was amazing to watch her creation take shape on the screen.

"This is great," said the head technician, admiring Marie's work. "What do you say we bring it to life?"

They went through to the 3D-printer rooms, where huge, thrumming machines turned the digital blueprints into solid parts. Once the components were ready and assembled, the technician took the glider through to the testing chambers, where crash-test dummies and frightening-looking cannons stood waiting to be used. The turbine fans were switched on to check how the air flowed over the glider's wings.

From behind Marie there came a loud, arrogant yawn. She spun around to see Ingrid scowling at her.

"This might be amazing to you newbies, but I've seen it all before," she drawled. "I'm bored. Bring on lunch."

Marie decided she wasn't going to let the sulky girl spoil her fun. Besides, she was probably a spy anyway, taking pictures with a secret camera.

As the tour wrapped up, Marie saw more astonishing inventions than she could count. Her favorite was a smart fabric that changed its color and pattern to match the setting you were in. Soldiers could use it for camouflage, while designers could use it for fashion. Marie loved the idea of walking through the park in the springtime and watching her outfit change to match the trees and flowers.

"One last stop, kids," Becca told them. She led them back into the pyramid and over to an elevator. Two

security guards in bulletproof vests and visored helmets stood by the elevator doors and checked Becca's ID before letting them through. Inside the elevator, two Robutlers watched the group closely with their red laser eyes.

"Top floor, please, Jenny," Becca told the elevator. The kids looked at one another and whispered excitedly. Becca nodded. "Yep. We're going to visit Mr. Vance's office."

The doors hissed open. More security guards and Robutlers challenged them. Once again, Becca had to show her ID. Then the guards checked everyone's V-bands.

"Nothing personal," a guard told Marie. "But we can't take risks with Mr. Vance's safety."

At long last, they passed through the doors and into Sterling Vance's personal office. But the great man

himself was nowhere to be seen.

There was a huge desk at one side, but he wasn't sitting behind it. Two Robutlers were guarding what looked like a bright-silver credit card on a pedestal, but he wasn't there either. He wasn't among the potted ferns, lounging in the black leather armchair, or hiding behind a huge, glossy white egg thing, which stood in the corner.

"Hellooo?" Jacques called. Marie nudged him.

Suddenly, the egg split in a single line from top to bottom. It swung open in two halves, letting out clouds of freezing fog. Out clambered a figure dressed in a white rubber suit and bulging blue goggles. Everyone shivered as the room suddenly became chilly.

"What are you all staring at?" laughed Vance. He pulled his goggles back, exposing his face. "Haven't you ever seen a cryo-cocoon before?"

Becca opened a window, and the fog began to drift out.

"What does it actually do, sir?" Jacques asked boldly.

"It's a brain supercharger! Puts your body into suspended animation so that your mind can go into overdrive. Ah, I see you're all wearing the V-bands I invented. Having fun with them?"

"Yes!" everyone burst out.

Marie noticed, to her surprise, that Becca was looking daggers at Vance. Maybe she didn't approve of him freezing his brain.

Vance sat casually on his desktop and launched into a question-and-answer session, choosing kids at random and letting them ask questions. Elisha asked him about his education, while Sophie asked him about the company's environmental policies. But Marie was desperately curious about the silver card on the pedestal.

She tried to catch Vance's eye, but he gave no sign that he recognized her, even though they had had a conversation outside her dorm room. *That makes sense,* she reasoned. She was meant to be working in secret, after all.

He spent a few minutes asking about their inventions and visions for the future, seeming genuinely interested. When he teased them about whether they'd be up for working at VanceCorp in the future, almost everyone rushed to say yes.

"Well, if that's all the questions, we'd better get you guys off to lunch." Vance slapped his thighs and moved to stand up.

"What's the silver card for?" Marie blurted out, as her curiosity finally got the best of her.

She heard Becca suck air sharply through her teeth. Suddenly the room went quiet.

Vance stood. Eyes narrowed, he crossed the room and stared right into Marie's eyes. "Why do you want to know?" His voice was colder than the gas from the cryo-cocoon.

Marie gulped. *Oh, no, he thinks I'm the spy.* She was suddenly sure she'd be flying back home to London on the next plane out of there. No way would Vance let her stay at the camp now. How was she going to explain this to her mum?

Vance slapped her on the shoulder and burst out laughing. "Gotcha! Of course you're allowed to ask questions. That's what science is all about! Oh, man. The look on your face!"

Sighs of relief came from all around. Especially from Marie.

"The silver card is my Alpha Key," said Vance. "It unlocks the special console that releases new Vance

system updates into the world. It's unique, of course. Only I get to use it."

A bell-like chime struck in the distance. Vance sat down and snapped his fingers. A staff member wearing a kimono and carrying a tray came hurrying out of the elevator. She pushed through the children, bowed to Vance and laid the tray down in front of him. It held a chrome teapot, a china cup and a pot of luminous green powder.

"Leave me now, young ones," said Vance. "It is the hour of tea and meditation."

"Hour of total fruitcake, more like," Sophie whispered in Marie's ear.

Vance poured himself some tea and sprinkled the green powder into it. "It's extracted from seaweed," he explained. "It stimulates the neurons." He sipped, and his face darkened. "Michelle!" he yelled to the woman who

had brought the tray in. "This tea is not heated to the correct temperature! How many times must I tell you?"

"Forgive me, Mr. Vance!" begged the woman.

"OK, gang. Tour's over. Let's go," Becca said briskly.

She ushered the kids out of the office, leaving Marie's head spinning. Was Sterling Vance a genius, or was he just a total weirdo? Or was he something even worse – a tyrant?

Chapter Six

Marie woke up to the sound of gentle chimes.

"Good morning, Marie. You are now awake," said Jenny.

"No kidding," Marie said and looked over to the other bed. Once again, Ingrid was nowhere in sight. Marie yawned and stretched happily. She felt under the pillow to check that her beloved notebook was still there. It was.

"You have slept for eight hours and seventeen minutes," said Jenny. "Local time is oh seven three oh hours. This represents a major improvement."

As Marie brushed her teeth, Jenny ran through the schedule for that day. "Nine a.m. to twelve noon, robotics class. Twelve noon to one p.m., lunch. One p.m. to four p.m., work on competition entries. Four p.m. to six p.m., rehearse for the talent show with Sophie. Six p.m. onward, campfire social at the private beach."

Marie splashed cold water on her face. Her groggy mind came into focus. "I have to build a robot," she told her reflection. "And catch a spy. But first, breakfast."

She met up with Gabby, Elisha and Sophie in the dining hall, where they were talking about a soccer game that had been on the night before. It was the most animated Marie had ever seen Elisha.

"I really love soccer," Elisha explained to Marie. "We're soccer fanatics in my family."

Marie didn't have time to respond to this new development as her V-band was flashing like crazy.

"We're late for robotics class!" she exclaimed and raced off to the Engineering Lab with the others in tow.

Marie recognized the teacher: it was Jesse, the ponytailed staff member who had registered their V-bands. "Come on in. Sit down, lie down if you like, whatever makes you comfortable," Jesse drawled.

Marie liked Jesse's laid-back approach. Lessons at school would be a lot more fun if she could spend them curled up in a beanbag!

Gabby put her hand up. "Excuse me, but isn't Becca our teacher?"

"Yeah, she's, like, meant to be, but I'm your substitute teacher today. Please don't lock me in the closet." Some of the kids laughed.

"So where's Becca?" Gabby insisted.

Jesse hesitated. "She's working on the Black Rose system upgrade. There are still a few teething problems

to work out. It's cool, though. Nothing we Vance engineers can't fix."

"Cool?" Gabby raised her eyebrow. "Isn't it due to release any day now?"

"Relax!" Jesse spread his fingers out, like he was miming a blooming flower. "The Black Rose upgrade will be ready on time, and you'll all get to play with it just like we promised! We'll get it done." He laughed nervously. "We want to keep our jobs, after all."

As a few late arrivals filed into the room and took their seats, Marie glanced over at Gabby suspiciously. How did her friend know when Black Rose was meant to be released? Obviously, she'd been hacking again. They were guests here at Vance campus, and Gabby was prying into the computer systems. The thought made Marie's stomach tie itself in queasy knots.

Could Gabby be the spy Vance was trying to catch?

She definitely had the skills for it. But she'd also boasted to Marie about those skills. That wasn't very stealthy. Unless it was a clever double bluff ...

"So we're going to go around the group now, and you guys can pitch me your designs," Jesse said. "Tell me about the robot you're planning to build, and why. Starting with ... you!"

He pointed right at Gabby. Marie wondered if he was paying her back for putting him on the spot before.

But Gabby wasn't rattled at all. "My robot's going to be called The Funkster," she said. "He's going to convert sound into movement."

"So he's a dancing robot?" Jesse said, doing a quick bit of body popping. "That rocks! OK, next?"

One by one, the camp kids explained what their robots would be. Marie grew more and more nervous. How had they all put so much thought into this? She'd

have to raise her game. She had to win this competition. If she lost her shot at the apprenticeship, it wasn't just her education at stake. Her mum's chance for a better life was on the line, too.

Sophie told everyone about the recycling robot she was planning. "Most cleaning robots just suck everything up, but that's wasteful. I'm introducing a sorting system, so anything that can be recycled goes to a separate container of its own."

Elisha was designing a soccer-themed robot. "Not a player," she explained. "My robot is a linesman. He can be totally unbiased and make sure everyone plays by the rules."

Ingrid gave Elisha a laser death stare, but Elisha didn't even blink. *Good for you*, Marie thought. Her friend was a lot tougher than she looked.

Jacques went next. "I am designing a robot de cuisine,"

he said solemnly. "He will be able to prepare simple dishes only." He grinned at Marie. "So he will cook about as well as the average British person."

"*Tsk.*" Marie folded her arms and gave him a scornful look. "You've never tried my peach cobbler." Then she laughed. So did Jesse and everyone else, apart from Ingrid.

Jacques gave Marie a little bow of mock respect. "In honor of my British friend, I shall call my robot Gordon RAM-stick." This time, everyone groaned.

Without being asked to speak, Ingrid stood up. "My robot will be called Steel Fist. He is a security guard. If he does not recognize your face, he will deliver a massive electric shock." She sat back down again to total silence.

"Way to kill the mood," muttered Jacques, rolling his eyes.

"OK, who else hasn't gone yet?" Jesse asked. He scanned the room and pointed at Marie. "We haven't heard from you."

Marie's mouth had suddenly gone dry. She looked around at all the expectant faces and tried to speak. "I, uh ... I haven't ... actually ... thought of a design yet." She gave them all a painful smile. "Sorry," she whispered.

Luckily, Becca came to her rescue. The engineer ran into the classroom just then. "Hi!" she gasped. "Sorry I'm late! OK, everyone, follow the arrows on your V-bands to the workshops. You've each got a bench to yourselves, and all the components you could possibly need. It's time to start bringing your designs to life!"

"And don't forget to sign up for the famous Vance Camp Talent Show," Jesse called after them as they emptied out of the classroom, babbling excitedly among themselves.

Marie cringed with embarrassment. She wasn't in any hurry to go to the workshops, as she had nothing to start working on. Elisha, Gabby and Sophie swept past her, caught up in the excitement, but Marie just looked down and dragged her feet.

"I wouldn't bother going to the workshop if I were you," said a familiar voice. "You haven't even got an idea, so what's the point?"

"Thanks, Ingrid," Marie said hollowly, without looking up. "That really helps, roomie."

Someone tapped her on the shoulder from behind. Marie spun around angrily, expecting to see Ingrid's smirking face again, but it was Becca.

"Hey, try not to worry," she said reassuringly. "There's still plenty of time to think of something."

"I hope so," Marie said.

"Ideas are tricky sometimes. You can't just snap your

fingers and get one. Just relax, keep an open mind, and something will come out of the blue when you least expect it."

Marie thought about that. All her best ideas had come to her when she was doing something completely different. It was a bit like how Izzy wouldn't ever come when he was called, but would always jump in her lap for a cuddle when Marie was trying to work on an invention.

"Thanks," she said, grinning.

"Any time, champ."

Jesse came hurrying up behind Becca. "Uh, can we talk?"

Marie carried on walking toward the workshops, but caught some of what Jesse was whispering to Becca.

"You were gone forever! I didn't have a lesson planned, so just asked them about their robots. Did you

fix the upgrade?"

"I didn't get rid of all the bugs. It's bad. It's worse than bad. Mr. V is going bananas. I thought he was going to fire me. Through the window."

"I guess we both might be looking for new jobs soon."

Becca shook her head. "These kids hero-worship him. But if they knew what he was really like..."

"Zip it, Becca. They might hear you."

I did hear you, thought Marie. *But I wish I hadn't...*

Chapter Seven

Later that week, Marie hurried out of the lab where she had spent the past hour doodling in her notebook, still desperately trying to come up with an idea for a robot. The rest of the campers had excitedly begun building theirs, but she wasn't any closer to an idea and she was finding it hard to concentrate after hearing Jesse and Becca's conversation. *Was Vance really that bad a boss?* She knew he was a tech genius, so why was Becca the one fixing the systems bugs?

Before she could think anymore about it, Sophie appeared beside her brandishing two rainbow-colored,

stripy lab coats.

"For the talent show," she chimed, beaming. "We've got to look the part to be the best magicians the camp's ever seen!"

Marie grimaced. "As long as you can make me disappear while wearing it, then I'm happy."

"You'll look great! Come on, let's go and practice."

The girls headed to Sophie and Elisha's room, where they'd been practicing their act for the past few days. They'd already designed the set and worked out the staging. They just needed a bit of practice getting the trick right. Timing was everything and Marie's timing was very off.

"Maybe I could add another bit into my 'mad scientist' routine?" Sophie suggested as Marie messed up the big reveal for the third time that afternoon.

"No, it's OK. I'll get it." Marie smiled sheepishly.

Sophie was a great showman and Marie wished it would rub off on her. *At least it's a distraction from designing a robot*, she thought. Rehearsing with Sophie reminded her that she was at camp to learn *and* have fun.

"Do you think I should tie lots of stationery in my hair to make me look more crazed?" asked Sophie, shoving pens into her ponytail, "I can use some of Elisha's clips to hold them in."

"Shouldn't you ask before you borrow Elisha's things?" Marie responded as Sophie started rummaging through Elisha's hair clips.

"Oh, she won't mind," replied Sophie, "I do it all the time."

Marie raised her eyebrows. She knew she wouldn't be happy with Ingrid going through her stuff, but then, she and Ingrid weren't friends. Maybe she'd feel

differently if she shared a room with Sophie or Elisha.

I wonder if Sophie makes a habit of rooting through other people's things.

The two friends rehearsed all afternoon until Gabby knocked on the door with Elisha and Jacques in tow.

"Come on, guys, you'll be late for the beach party," Gabby said, waving her towel in the air. "I want to go swimming before they start making the s'mores."

VanceCorp's private beach was almost too perfect to be real. The sand glimmered like powdered gold in the setting sun, without a piece of litter anywhere in sight. The waves, blue as laundry detergent, came rolling in to shore as smoothly as sine curves on a graph. The air smelled clean and somehow electric.

Marie's skin tingled. She felt more awake and alive than she had in weeks.

"Now I really feel like I'm in California!" Marie said, adjusting the settings on her glasses to "shades" mode. The lenses shifted from colored to dark.

"Hope you all like to sing," said Gabby, setting her guitar down carefully on a tartan blanket, next to a big bag of marshmallows. "I don't like to go solo."

"Shall we play beach soccer?" suggested Jacques, bouncing a soccer ball from knee to knee.

"Sure!" called Gabby, and she and Sophie ran to join him. Marie started to follow, but noticed Elisha was still standing shyly by their bags.

"Are you going to play, Elisha?" she asked.

"OK," she replied, looking pleased that she hadn't been forgotten in the excitement.

The friends split into two teams: Gabby and Jacques

versus Marie and Elisha. Sophie volunteered to be the referee. She blew the whistle and the game began in a flurry of kicked-up sand. Marie liked being on Elisha's team. Although she'd been quiet in all their classes, Elisha was much more confident playing soccer.

Elisha also turned out to be a pro goalie. Every shot Jacques and Gabby took, Elisha saved. She knew exactly which way to dive to catch the ball, even when Jacques tried to trick her by aiming to the right of the goal but kicking to the left at the last second.

"How are you doing that?" Marie asked, after Elisha had saved her second goal in a row.

"It's easy," replied Elisha, "You just estimate the angle of the ball to the goal and the speed at which Jacques will kick it, and then you know exactly where it will go."

Marie stared at her openmouthed.

Elisha blushed. "Math is ... kind of my thing," she explained.

Wow, thought Marie. *Elisha is a math genius!*

The game continued, with Elisha saving two more goals until Gabby scored one. Determined to score his own goal, Jacques kicked the ball from the far side of the playing area.

"Jacques, that was definitely offside!" Elisha called as Jacques kicked the ball past her into the makeshift goal.

"No it wasn't! Zhere is no way that I was offside," he protested.

"You're not even standing on the field! The line is *there*." Elisha pointed at the smudged line Jacques had drawn earlier.

"No, the line is *zhere*," Jacques replied, pointing to a

line farther from the goal. "It's up to our ref to decide. Zophie?"

"I don't know," shrugged Sophie, looking from Jacques to Elisha as they continued to bicker.

"I didn't know you were so good at soccer, Elisha," Marie said, in an attempt to break up the bickering. "How did you learn to play so well?"

"Oh, I'm not really very good." Elisha noticed the friends were all looking at her, and turned away.

Sensing Elisha wanted a break from the attention, Marie kicked the ball toward Jacques. "Check out my trick shot!" she called.

But Jacques wasn't paying attention. The ball went flying over Jacques, Gabby, and Sophie's heads and hit a nearby sunbather.

Oh no! thought Marie, running over to the person she'd hit. "I'm so sorr—"

"You *should* be sorry, you idiot!"

The injured sunbather rolled over, clutching the ball. It was Ingrid. "Is it not enough that you are terrible at robotics? You have to be incompetent at soccer also?"

"I'm really sorry that I hit you, Ingrid," Marie said. "It won't happen again."

"I know it won't," Ingrid snarled. She stood up and kicked the ball out into the sea.

"Hey!" shouted Gabby and Sophie in unison.

"There was no need to do that," Elisha reasoned. "Marie said sorry."

"It wasn't good enough," huffed Ingrid. She turned and sauntered over to the campfire, kicking sand at the friends on her way.

"I'm sorry, guys," Marie apologized.

"Don't worry," replied Elisha. "Ingrid is just bitter. I bet she's rubbish at soccer."

Marie smiled gratefully. It was nice to see Elisha come out of her shell. She'd been so confident when playing soccer and had even stood up to Ingrid. It was so strange compared to how quiet she usually was at camp.

Wait, thought Marie. *Could Elisha be the spy?*

After all the campers had gathered around the fire, Gabby pulled out her guitar.

"Let's sing some campfire songs," she suggested.

"Great idea," said Becca, "who wants to start?"

Several campers put their hands up, but before Becca could choose one of them Jacques started singing *Despacito* at the top of his voice.

Gabby looked at Marie and rolled her eyes. *Trust Jacques to want the spotlight.*

Jacques caught the girls looking at each other and winked, singing louder and even more out of tune.

Suddenly, Marie's phone started ringing. Her dad's name flashed up on screen.

Relieved to have an excuse to get away from Jacques' terrible singing, she got up, staggered away from the campfire and answered.

"Hey, Marie!" said her dad down a crackling phone line. "How's camp?"

"It's fun, Dad. I've made some friends, but ..."

"But?"

Marie sighed. "There's a robot-building competition. And I'm struggling to think of an idea."

"That's OK, darling! I know you'll come up with something," her dad said immediately. "Hey, remember when you couldn't decide what to do at the school science competition? You wanted to build a skateboard that was powered by kinetic energy AND Rollerblades with jet packs."

Marie laughed. "True."

"So what did you do? You combined the ideas. That's how you created the Marie Curious hoverboard."

Marie grinned at the memory. That invention had been fun, even if the hoverboard had gone AWOL and flown off, knocking down the neighbor's fence. Talking to her dad always made her feel better.

"That was funny! Mum said that as long as we had neighbors, I was only allowed to make inventions that stuck to the ground after that," she giggled.

"Ha! That sounds like your mum," he chuckled. "Anyway, my love, I have to go ... *chk* ... the line's cutting ou—"

The phone went dead. Marie was used to this by now. Reception was never very good in the middle of the North Sea.

She smiled to herself as she remembered building

the hoverboard with her dad. They'd spent several weekends in her Inventing Shed, trying to work out how to make it fly...

Marie froze.

That's it! she thought, smiling to herself. Finally, she had her idea!

Chapter Eight

"You've got bags under your eyes. Have you been staying up late again?" Marie's mum frowned.

"I've been working!" Marie held her V-band up in front of her open notebook, so her mum could see the design sketches.

Marie had hardly slept at all, but there was no point telling her mum that. She'd been sketching in her bed capsule since she'd come back from the campfire the previous night, finally going to sleep around midnight. In the morning, she'd woken up before dawn and carried on where she had left off. The moment the design was

complete, she'd made a video phone call back home.

"What is it? Some sort of bird robot?"

"I'm calling her Eagle Eye," Marie said.

The robot in her sketches had sleek wings with rotors that could swivel backward, allowing it to swoop as well as hover on the spot. Its head was a camera mounted on a flexible neck. In the center of its body were two grabbing claws on extendable rodlike legs.

"Next time you drop something, you won't need to call Kate," Marie explained. "All you'll have to do is open up your V-band, look through Eagle Eye's camera, tap on the thing you want her to pick up, and she'll do it for you!"

"That sounds great, until Izzy decides to box her," laughed Marie's mum. "Your Eagle Eye won't pick Izzy up and drop him down the chimney, will she?"

"Safety features will come as standard," Marie said,

grinning from ear to ear.

She felt so much better now that she actually had an idea for a robot. Becca had been right; inspiration had struck out of the blue.

And knowing that Eagle Eye could make a difference to her mum's life was the best feeling of all. Even if she didn't win the competition, she'd still have that.

"OK. I'm going out shopping. Don't mess around, love. Work hard," said Marie's mum.

"Don't worry. I will!"

The campers had an intensive science class again that morning. The idea was to learn as much as you could in as short a time as possible, by combining lectures, demonstrations and hands-on experiments. This meant that every student could get the maximum benefit, no matter what their learning style was.

Today's session was focused on materials. Marie got

to blast ceramic tiles with a flamethrower, to simulate a space shuttle's scorching descent through Earth's atmosphere. Gabby refracted light through a huge prism. Sophie used a vial of nanobots to "digest" some plastic cups and jumped up and down with glee when they were reduced to their base elements. Elisha and Jacques got to play with ferrofluids.

"This stuff is amazing," Jacques said, scooping out a beaker full of what looked like inky black soup. "A liquid that reacts to magnetic fields!"

Elisha held it over a powerful electromagnet and they all watched rubbery-looking spikes form out of the fluid. Marie stared, amazed. It was the closest you could come to actually seeing a magnetic field.

"It's beautiful!" she sighed.

Jacques sighed too. "Yes, Marie, mon amour. It is even more beautiful than you." He leaned down until his lips

were almost brushing the spikes, as if he was going to give it a kiss.

"Don't!" Elisha cried, but it was too late.

Jacques's face suddenly smacked down into the fluid and stayed there.

"Turn it off!" he gurgled. "Turn it off!"

Elisha flicked the electromagnet switch. Jacques came back up, gasping, his face covered with dripping black liquid. "Forgot all about my braces," he told them. "They got stuck to the ferrofluid."

Marie couldn't help but laugh. Jacques was ridiculously handsome, but he was such a clown it helped you not to notice.

"Let's get to lunch," Gabby said. "Something pretty special's coming down the pipe."

"What do you mean?" Marie asked, wondering if Gabby was talking about the lunch menu.

"We're testing the new VanceOS update at noon today! Black Rose. I can't wait to check out those new special features!"

Gabby had hardly touched her burger and fries. She kept checking her V-band for the time. "Eleven fifty-one ... eleven fifty-two ... come on, come on!"

Marie, who had demolished half a pizza, was starting to get excited too. Gabby's enthusiasm was catching.

"What features are you guys looking forward to most?" asked Sophie, who had joined them late.

"Definitely augmented reality," Marie said. "I can't believe that's going to be standard on Vance devices!"

"Not all devices," Gabby muttered, still staring at her V-band. "Just the ones here on the campus. This is a local

beta test, OK? The rest of the world won't get the update until Vance releases it officially."

"Using his Alpha Key," added Marie, remembering what they'd learned in Sterling Vance's office.

"Well, we're getting it, and that's what matters to me," said Sophie cheerfully.

"Nice to be first," Elisha agreed.

Gabby grabbed Marie's arm. "Eleven fifty-three. The download's starting. This is it!"

"Attention," Jenny said over the PA system. "All Vance devices are now installing the Black Rose update, beta version. Your views count! Please give all feedback to your supervisor. Enjoy the features, including the new 3D HoloJenny. I look forward to meeting you in person."

Cheers broke out all across the dining hall. The girls forgot about their meals and watched the install bar

creep across their V-band screens.

"Almost there," Marie whispered. "Almost..."

INSTALLATION COMPLETE, read every screen.

There was a moment of total silence as everyone held their breath in anticipation.

And then the shouts and screams began.

"What's going on?" Marie gasped.

"Look!" Elisha pointed across the hall. The screaming was coming from a group of employees in the line for food. The robot servers weren't putting the food on their plates. They were putting it on *them*.

"Enjoy your meal!" said one robot as it poured beans over a startled young technician. Another robot pelted the lady next in line with pizza slices. Nearby, every different flavor of soda poured out of a drink machine, and at the dessert station a machine was pumping out a steady stream of chocolate frozen yogurt.

"Is this one of the new features?" asked Sophie, confused.

"I don't think so," said Marie. "Look outside!"

Out on the lawns, chaos had broken loose. The water sprinklers were gushing like fountains and whirling like Catherine wheels. A robotic lawn mower was carving a path through the flower beds, sending petals spraying everywhere. Two drones crashed in midair and promptly exploded.

A warning siren began to blare. The fire sprinklers went off and gushed water down on the dining hall. People yelled in alarm, some running out of the room, some hiding under the tables. Marie stood, her baby hairs fuzzing to a halo around her dripping face, struggling to think of what she could do to help. It was complete chaos.

"Gabby, we've got to do something!" Marie yelled.

"Everything running VanceOS is going crazy," Gabby yelled back.

"Yeah, I noticed!"

A Robutler came veering madly in Marie's direction. It wasn't slowing down. She grabbed a lunch tray and walloped it as hard as she could. It went spinning off, crashed through a window and landed in the fountain.

"Nice one," called Elisha, booting another out-of-control Robutler with a goal kick.

Marie forced herself to think clearly. "We need to get everyone to safety," she said. "Somewhere there isn't any tech."

"There's nowhere without tech! This is Vance campus!" Elisha replied.

"Yes there is," Marie said, remembering their tour. She stood on a table. "Everyone, follow me! I know what to do!"

With Gabby, Elisha and Sophie following, Marie ran out of the room. A growing train of people followed her. Every corridor they ran through was a scene of mayhem, with offices flooded with fire-retardant foam, screens displaying a riot of shifting colors and blaring noise, and escalators going the wrong way at triple speed.

Marie finally found the corridor she was looking for. She pushed open the double doors that led to the Zen Garden and led everyone inside. There was none of the chaos here at all, just plants, stillness, stones and sand.

"Good call, Marie," said Jacques.

"Yeah," Gabby said approvingly. "I'd forgotten this place existed. No tech anywhere."

Becca emerged from the crowd of people. "Now that I can hear myself think, I might be able to fix this." She sat down cross-legged, flipped open a slim silver laptop and began to type at blinding speed.

A holo-image of a woman with short black hair, silver skin and flickering emerald eyes appeared in the air in front of her. "Hello, Becca," it said, and Marie recognized Jenny's familiar voice. "You have been granted emergency access to my local systems. Please enter your command."

"Jenny, remove Black Rose and go back to the previous version!"

"Are you sure? Uninstalling Black Rose will remove several exciting special features—"

"Just do it!" Becca yelled, and pounded the keys.

HoloJenny vanished. Marie clenched her fists in anticipation. Seconds later, Jenny's voice came from Becca's laptop. "Black Rose has been successfully uninstalled."

Becca sank back and wiped her forehead. "Oh, thank goodness."

Marie ran to the window. The robot lawn mower had gone back to mowing the grass in straight lines instead of attacking the flowers. The sprinklers had stopped spraying. Judging by the cheers that came from outside the Zen Garden, the rest of the Vance campus was returning to normal, too.

As people began to congratulate Becca and call her a hero, Marie suddenly realized how big a deal Black Rose really was. Almost every household had Vance devices in it – phones, televisions, computers, even fridges – and they were all running VanceOS. Every last one.

If Black Rose was released without the bugs being fixed, then the exact same chaos would break out all over the world ...

Chapter Nine

Now that her design for the robot competition was complete, it was time to start building. Marie was a little worried about how she was going to turn Eagle Eye from a design on a page in her notebook into a real robot. She was pretty complicated. *Am I supposed to build her from scratch?* she wondered.

Luckily, the Vance engineers were on hand to help. Instead of a random assortment of scrounged-together bits and pieces from her Inventing Shed, Marie had access to every single gadget and component Vance had ever made. All she had to do was tap in an order on

her V-band, and the parts would be delivered to her in minutes. Soon she had a huge haul of rotors, electronic circuits and cables to play with.

"But what if I need something that doesn't exist yet?" she asked Becca.

"That's what the 3D printers are for," Becca said, smiling. "Remember that glider you made? Just custom build the part you need in the virtual design studio, and let the printers bring it to life."

So that was how Marie designed the body and wings for Eagle Eye. Working in virtual reality was a weird feeling at first, but you soon got used to it. Marie felt like a ribbon dancer, tracing elegant neon lines through the air with her handheld controllers.

Sure enough, later that same afternoon, a drone came whizzing up to her workstation carrying a parcel. Marie eagerly ripped it open and took out a set of smooth,

golden, streamlined pieces. It was Eagle Eye, just like she'd drawn her on the page, all ready to be assembled.

Later, as she was fine-tuning Eagle Eye's balance, her V-band dinged. "Good evening, Marie," said Jenny. "This is your reminder to attend the talent show tonight at seven."

Marie grinned. "I hadn't forgotten!" She and Sophie had been rehearsing their comedy magic act during every spare moment they had. Marie couldn't wait to show it off, even though she still wasn't fond of their rainbow-striped outfits!

"I wish I could go," Becca groaned. She was starting to look haggard and worn out. "I could so use a break."

"Still fixing the bugs in Black Rose?" Marie guessed.

"Doing my best. But as soon as I squish one, two more pop up."

From across the room, Ingrid announced, "Well, I'm

not going to the show. It sounds lame, and I've got a robot to finish."

"Hey, Ingrid, did you hear that?" Gabby cupped a hand to her ear. "That was the sound of nobody asking for your opinion!"

Marie sneaked a look at Ingrid's robot, Steel Fist, on the way out of the lab. It was looking pretty scary already, with a metal skull on top like the one from Vance's welcome presentation and thick arms with jagged clamping hands. Thank goodness the robots didn't have to fight each other because Steel Fist would definitely win!

Sterling Vance had set aside a small lecture hall for the talent show, complete with a stage. It was much cozier

than the huge auditorium and Marie felt a lot more comfortable there. The seats were packed with excited campers and staff members.

Marie peeped through the curtains and saw that even Mr. Vance himself had joined them, sitting in the very back row. He was dressed in the same charcoal-gray suit and tinted glasses he'd been wearing when he had visited her room.

Jesse, who was acting as MC, welcomed the audience and told a few terrible jokes. Then it was showtime!

The first act to perform, Marie and Sophie headed through the curtains, into a storm of applause. Marie's heart thumped with nerves. "Good evening, everyone!" she said. "Professor Sophie and I would like to show you our latest experiment."

"My lab assistant and I have been working on something not even Mr. Vance has attempted," said

Sophie. "Teleportation!"

The curtains rolled back and revealed Marie and Sophie's hastily assembled props. Two tall boxes covered in aluminum foil stood on the left and right sides of the stage. Between them was a table covered in scientific equipment, which Jesse had helped them scavenge.

"Are you ready?" asked Sophie.

"Yes, Professor," Marie said, and bowed.

Marie opened the left-hand capsule, wriggled inside, shut the door and fastened it. As Sophie kept up the patter outside, Marie reached down to the service hatch in the floor. It took only seconds to pull it up, crawl under the stage, cross over to where the second pod was positioned and let herself up into it.

Meanwhile, Sophie was pulling levers, pressing buttons and laughing manically like a mad scientist. Brilliant flashes of light lit up the stage.

"Transmission complete! Now let's see if she survived the trip." Sophie flung open the second pod.

Marie jumped out. "Ta-da!"

The curtains closed, with the audience cheering and roaring for more.

When they went backstage, Elisha gave them both a hug. "That was brilliant!" she said. "You looked so funny in your costumes and the audience loved it!"

"Not everyone. Did you see Vance? He wasn't even smiling," said Sophie.

Marie passed Elisha her soccer ball. "Don't worry about him. You're up next, Elisha. Break a leg."

Elisha went onstage and demonstrated her fancy footwork with flicks, tricks and keepie-uppies. Jacques performed a hilarious comedy routine, his impressions of famous stars all the more impressive considering English wasn't his native language. All the rest of

the acts were up to the same standard. The moment each performer finished, the audience whooped and applauded. The only person who didn't seem to be enjoying himself was Vance. He just sat watching the show impassively, without a trace of a smile. Marie wondered if he was just saving up his energy and would eventually bound onto the stage to sing "My Way" or do some weird dance ritual.

Gabby brought her robot, Funkster, onto the stage for the final act. "Are you ready to get down?" she said into the microphone. "Funkster, gimme a beat!"

Funkster's eyes flashed. He blasted out a rhythm. Some of the kids in the audience began to clap along.

"This song's inspired by the periodic table of elements," announced Gabby.

But as she launched into her rap, Funkster's head suddenly exploded.

A horrible screech of feedback made everyone wince. The beat suddenly cut off, and Gabby was left coughing in a cloud of smoke.

"Looks like I've got some repair work to do," she said, fanning the air in front of her face.

Much, much later, following the after-party, Marie let herself back into her room. She'd had an amazing time dancing with her new friends.

As she snuggled down in bed, still too excited to sleep, she wished there was someone she could chat to about the show and party. But Ingrid's bed capsule was closed, and the sound of snoring came from inside it.

Marie sighed. Her last thought before sleep claimed her was: *Why couldn't I have gotten someone nice for a roommate?*

Chapter Ten

The next morning, when Marie arrived at the Engineering Lab, her notebook was gone.

Her first thought was that she must have accidentally buried it under her ever-growing pile of robot parts. But digging through those revealed nothing. Was it in the drawer? No. Had it fallen down the back of the workbench? Again, no.

Her frustration began to turn into real panic. The notebook had all her notes for Eagle Eye in it. She wasn't even sure she'd be able to put her together properly without it.

"Something wrong?" Ingrid smirked at Marie from across the room.

With that, she got it. "You should know!" Marie raged. This was too much. Marie had had enough of being polite. Ingrid wasn't shy – she was evil!

Ingrid blinked slowly. "What do you mean?"

"You stole my notebook, you snaky—"

"No I didn't!" Ingrid shrieked. "How dare you accuse me!"

Marie, to her horror, saw Ingrid reach for Steel Fist's activation switch. The guard robot crackled with electricity. *It's going to zap me!* Marie thought in alarm.

"Hey, hey, calm down!" Becca said in soothing tones, gripping her cup of coffee like a protective shield. "Let's keep it civil, guys. You'll give me a headache."

Ingrid backed off, keeping her eyes locked on Marie. "I am not a thief," she snarled.

"Then where's my notebook?"

"How should I know? Why would I want that grubby old thing?"

"OK, enough! Time-out!" Becca winced and held up a hand. Marie was struck by how tired the camp counselor looked – she had bags under her eyes and her hair was stringy and unwashed. "Marie, I'm sure your notebook will turn up. Ingrid, Marie's clearly upset, so give her some space. Both of you, focus on your robots."

Marie did her best, but it wasn't easy. She could feel Ingrid's hateful glare boring into her like a drill. Without her notebook, she didn't dare put any of Eagle Eye's parts together permanently, in case she assembled her wrong. She had to settle for test fitting them, which felt like a waste of time.

"Argh!" Elisha yelled at her robot from the next workbench along. "What's your problem? Why won't

128

you just do what you're supposed to?"

"Sounds like the whole lab is cursed this morning," Marie said. She put Eagle Eye's parts away and went to help Elisha. If she couldn't get anything useful done on her own robot, at least she could help a friend.

Elisha's robot linesman was only half a meter tall. He looked a little like the planet Saturn, with a round ball in the middle surrounded by a disk. The disk stayed level, while the ball rolled him around wherever he needed to go.

"What's the problem?" Marie asked.

"See for yourself," said Elisha. She set her robot down on the floor and gave two shrill blows on her referee's whistle, which was the robot's cue to switch itself on.

His head lit up. His motors whirred into action. But instead of zooming smoothly down the space between the workbenches, he veered left and charged right into the bench. Elisha moaned and shook her fists. Her robot

wobbled off in a different direction and hit another desk.

"How's he supposed to be a linesman if he can't go in a straight line?" Elisha snatched the robot up and peered at him.

Marie thought of the cart on the plane. "You've checked his drive wheels?"

"Of course." Elisha sighed. "I'll just have to strip him down piece by piece. That's time I can't afford to lose!"

"I'll help," Marie volunteered. Elisha gave her a grateful smile.

Together they unscrewed the robot's casing, spun his drive wheels around, tested his motor and even replaced his battery. But he still lurched about like an overexcited puppy.

"Maybe he needs more light?" Marie suggested. "It might be too dark in here for him to see properly."

Elisha froze. "Wait a minute," she said. She reached

down to the robot's camera eye. A single piece of black tape was stuck over it.

Marie couldn't believe it. "We spent the whole morning trying to find the problem, and it was just a bit of tape?"

"It must be my fault. I was careless."

"I don't think so," Marie said darkly. "Look."

Ingrid wasn't looking at them, but there was no mistaking the smug smile on her face. And there was a roll of black duct tape on her workbench.

"So, it was sabotage," Elisha hissed. "First your notebook, and now this. She'll do anything to win. Ooh, I'd like to wipe that smile off her face!"

"Maybe we can," said Marie.

"How? We'd have to prove it was her."

Marie began to smile. "Don't worry. I've got an idea."

During free time, Marie found Gabby relaxing in the Vance beauty salon, which – like everything else on the campus – was staffed by robots. "Chica!" Gabby said, calling Marie over. "You've got to try the robo-manicure. Check out my nails."

The beautician robot was using a fan-assisted titanium clipper, which sucked up the little slivers of fingernail as quickly as they were cut. Gabby selected her look from a tablet, the fake nails were instantly printed out from liquid acrylic, and the beautician used a tiny airbrush to apply the coating.

Gabby held her hand up, and a holographic rainbow shimmered across her fingertips like the haze from sprinklers in the sunshine. "Laser nails," she said,

grinning. "And tomorrow morning, I can get a totally different style!"

"Cool," Marie said.

Gabby frowned. "Cool? Is that it? OK, mi amiga, something's on your mind. What's up?"

"We should probably talk in private," Marie said, looking around nervously. She didn't want any Vance employees to overhear what she had to say.

Ten minutes later, Marie sat nestled in a beanbag in Gabby's room while her friend paced up and down.

"You want me to hack into the VanceCorp security system? The actual video camera archives? Just how good do you think I am, Marie?"

"Sorry." Marie squirmed, aware she'd put her friend in an uncomfortable position. "If it's too hard for you—"

"Did I say that?" Gabby snapped. "Pass me that laptop. I'm going in."

Marie crossed her fingers for luck as Gabby typed, muttered and typed some more. Suddenly, she reared back from her laptop with a triumphant shout.

"I got access! But we've got to be quick. What do you need?"

Marie pointed at a folder labeled ENGINEERING LAB WEST. "This one. Try and find last night, while we were at the talent show."

In a flurry of clicks, Gabby brought up the video footage. It showed a view through the security camera. Ingrid was the only one in the lab. Marie felt a delicious thrill. *I've got you*, she thought.

As they watched, Ingrid glanced around to make sure she was all alone, then ran across to Elisha's workbench. Marie punched her hand into her palm as she saw Ingrid stick the tape over the linesman robot's camera eye. "There's our proof," she murmured. "Now watch her

steal my notebook."

But to her surprise, Ingrid ran out of the lab, leaving Marie's notebook untouched.

"Weird," Gabby said. "Maybe she came back for it." She skipped ahead ten minutes. The notebook was still there. The time read 19:12.

As they watched, the footage flickered. Digital static fizzed across the screen. It cleared again, just as abruptly, but now the time read 21:12.

"Your notebook disappeared!" Gabby said.

"So did two hours of camera footage," Marie exclaimed. "Someone deleted it!"

"It must have been Ingrid, coming back for your notebook," Gabby said.

"I don't think so, or she'd have deleted the first bit, too. It's got to be someone else."

Gabby hastily closed the connection. Marie took

a deep breath. They looked at one another. In that moment, Marie made a decision.

"Gabby, I have to tell you something. Promise you won't tell a soul."

"OK." Gabby raised an eyebrow.

"Sterling Vance came to see me in secret just after I arrived. He told me there's a spy here. One of us campers. He wanted me to be on the lookout, but I wasn't to tell anyone else."

Gabby's eyes widened and her hands went to her mouth. She whispered, "He told me the exact same thing!"

Neither of them said it, but the same thought burned in both their minds: *Could the mysterious spy have stolen Marie's notebook?*

Marie was determined to find out the truth. They didn't call her Marie Curious for nothing!

Marie slept uneasily that night. She didn't trust her roommate, but she couldn't do anything about it without getting Gabby into trouble for hacking. She woke up too late for breakfast and had to grab some noodles from a vending machine on the way to class. Chemistry, her V-band told her.

The route to the chemistry lab took her past Engineering. She was already late, but Eagle Eye's safety was preying on her mind. Ingrid might not have stolen the notebook, but she had definitely sabotaged Elisha's robot. It was worth checking on Eagle Eye, just to make sure she was OK.

Marie let herself into the Engineering Lab. There was her workstation, seemingly undisturbed. There was

Eagle Eye. And there was her notebook, slap bang in the middle of all her bits and pieces.

She stared at it. *Am I going mad?* She ran over, picked it up and leafed through it. None of the pages had been torn out. It was exactly as it should be.

"Is someone trying to mess with my head?" she asked herself aloud.

Nobody answered. On impulse, Marie flipped the notebook over. There, on the back cover, was a new stain – a green splodge. Either her eyes were playing tricks on her, or it was glowing faintly.

No time to worry about that now. She was seriously late.

Marie crashed into the chemistry session, flustered and out of breath. The other campers, already in goggles and lab coats, all looked at her with concern. The instructor, a woman Marie didn't recognize, wordlessly

directed her to the equipment lockers.

"What are we studying?" Marie whispered, pulling on her safety gloves. "Acids? Explosives?"

"Fizzy drinks," Sophie told her.

"As I was saying," the instructor smiled sweetly, "VanceCorp is extending its range of energy beverages that supercharge both brain and body. Today, you campers are going to help us brew them up."

After an explanation of what makes fizzy drinks fizzy – carbon dioxide gas, as Marie already knew – they were allowed to go and experiment in groups, which gave Marie a chance to tell her friends about her mysterious reappearing notebook.

"What do you think this could be?" She showed them the glowing stain.

"Sophie?" Gabby said. "You're good at biology. Any ideas?"

Sophie frowned. "If I had a microscope, I could probably tell you."

Elisha silently tapped her on the shoulder and pointed. Sophie rolled her eyes. "Duh. Of course. We're in a science lab. There are microscopes right here!"

The girls huddled around, forming a screen, as Sophie used the microscope to zoom in on Marie's notebook. "Hmm," Sophie said. "I don't recognize the cell structure. If I had to guess, I'd say it's some sort of marine plant."

"Oh my gosh," Gabby said, snapping her fingers. "I know where I've seen that color before. Remember 'the hour of tea and meditation'?"

"It's the seaweed stuff Sterling Vance sprinkled on his tea!" Marie exclaimed.

The instructor was coming. Sophie quickly shoved the notebook back into Marie's hands.

Marie's mind swirled with questions. Could Sterling

Vance have taken her notebook? Why would a tech genius like him be interested in her designs? Besides, wasn't he at the talent show at the time the notebook had gone missing?

It didn't make any sense. Sophie winked at Marie as she stirred a beaker of cherry-colored liquid, and Marie winked back.

In a horrible flash, she suddenly thought: *What if Sophie is the spy?*

The Australian girl was so friendly. Could that just be a front? Marie only had Sophie's word that the stain was Vance's tea. If she were the spy, surely she'd be trying to pin the blame on someone else.

Something fishy was definitely going on. Marie shook her head and tried to concentrate. The spy hunt was too much of a distraction. For now, she had to focus on winning the robotics competition. Because she'd gotten

started later, everyone was way ahead of her and there were only four more days to go ...

Chapter Eleven

"It's paradise," Jacques said, sighing.

Jesse had just let them into the Games Development building, which was brand-new. "With the new Black Rose update coming out, Vance is planning a big push into virtual reality and augmented reality gaming," Jesse explained. "We thought you guys might like to try out some of the hardware."

The gaming rigs in front of them were sleek, black and humming with power. Each unit had a helmet on it, like something an alien pilot might wear.

"Everyone, take a seat and put your helmets on," said

Jesse. "I have to warn you, being in virtual reality can be overwhelming. You can get carsick in a virtual car just as easily as a real one. So if you don't feel good, take the helmet off right away."

The helmet fitted snugly over Marie's head and face. It was a bit like wearing a scuba diving mask. She found herself apparently standing on a simple racetrack. Letters that looked like they were molded out of liquid metal appeared in front of her, reading GET READY. A pounding bass track began to play.

This wasn't anything like the VR design studio she'd already tried out. This experience was meant to get your heart pounding and set your nerves on fire.

"First world: Formula One. Reach in front of you for your controller and have fun!" said Jenny's voice in her ear.

A virtual controller suddenly appeared in Marie's lap.

She reached for it with her real hands, and found she was holding a real controller. As she moved it around, the virtual one moved too. Her brain was completely convinced she was inside the computer-generated world.

Before her eyes, the graphics morphed, becoming sharper and sharper until they were photo-realistic. Marie's mouth fell open. She was, somehow, now standing – no, sitting – in the middle of a racetrack. The sun glinted off windows and car exhausts. There were even people waving from the grandstand!

Marie began to feel a little nervous. What if a car came roaring around the corner and ran her down?

Suddenly, little shining sparks appeared all around her. They began to trace lines, sketching out a dashboard, a windshield, a steering wheel. The empty spaces between the lines became solid. Marie watched

as the car built itself around her. Even the engine was there, superbly detailed, like an X-ray. Now her hands appeared, but they were covered with leather racing gloves.

A voice announced, "Three, two, one ..." and the deafening roar of car engines erupted all around her. Marie swallowed hard and pulled the accelerator trigger.

"This is insane," she whispered. "I don't know how to drive!"

Her stomach churned. Cars were whizzing past her. She glanced in her mirror and saw another driver coming up hard behind. She swerved to avoid them, skidding over the edge of the racetrack and into the gravel. Clenching her teeth, she revved her engine again. The other driver shot past and waved at her. It was Ingrid.

All of Marie's muscles tensed like piano strings. She

was starting to sweat inside the helmet. She swung around another corner and the virtual sunlight dazzled her eyes. Why did it have to be so realistic? This was supposed to be fun, but Marie felt trapped. She fought the urge to rip the headset off.

There was Ingrid up ahead. Marie piled on the revs and came barreling down at her roommate. "Got you now," she growled.

Without warning, the racetrack exploded into a storm of wild pixels. Marie plunged through pure chaos for a few seconds before the scenery snapped back into a new form. Now she was sitting in a roller coaster car, clunking steadily toward the crest of a massive drop. She seemed to be in an amusement park built into the side of a mountain.

Her mouth watered. She felt like she needed to burp.

"Second world: Death Drop Mountain," cooed Jenny.

Marie made the mistake of looking over the edge. The roller coaster track was high up, mounted on rickety-looking wooden pillars. She moaned as the carriage came closer and closer to the big drop. "Good thing this is only virtual," she muttered to herself, "because it'd get shut down if this was real!"

She could see every weathered plank in the track, and they looked none too sturdy. Her stomach flipped like a pancake as they crested the rise, tipped over and began to drop down, down, down—

Marie yanked the helmet up off her head. Sweat ran down the back of her neck. Her hands were shaking. She was back in the good old solid ordinary world.

But her stomach hadn't caught up yet. It gurgled and sloshed like someone rinsing out a mop in a bucket. The thought catapulted Marie to her feet. Her chair fell over.

"You OK?" Jesse asked, hurrying to her side.

"Feel sick," Marie said, covering her mouth with her hand and holding her stomach.

"Bathrooms are down the hall." Another camper was waving his hand for help. Jesse went to see to him, leaving Marie to cope alone.

"Wheee!" Elisha shouted underneath her helmet. "Let's go faster!"

At least someone's having fun, Marie thought as she pushed through the door and stumbled down the corridor. She blundered past an ornamental fern and miserably wondered if she could throw up in its vase if she didn't find the bathroom fast enough.

This wasn't a building she'd ever been in before. Jesse's vague instructions didn't help much, either. How far "down the hall" was she meant to go? Every junction looked exactly like the last. This place was all sterile white walls, electric-blue carpets and closed office doors.

She finally found a sign that read EXECUTIVE WASHROOM, and groaned. Either Jesse had given directions without thinking, or she'd overshot. Well, her stomach wasn't about to let her wait a second longer. Executive or not, she was going in.

Marie stood at the sink and splashed cold water on her face. These were some classy bathrooms, with little lavender soap bars, posh hand cream and fluffy towels. She was still wobbly, but beginning to feel better.

"Pull yourself together, Marie," she told her reflection.

She turned to leave, only to hear a familiar voice coming from the corridor outside. It was Becca, and she sounded furious. "Come on, Vance," she said. "Pick up, or so help me ..."

I'm not supposed to be in here, Marie thought in a moment of panic. She hurled herself into an open stall and quickly locked the door.

The door opened and Becca's heels clicked on the marble floor. Marie, filled with irresistible curiosity, peered under the stall door and watched Becca's feet pace back and forth. She could hear the silvery trill of a V-band call trying to connect. Then came the soft ding of a call commencing.

Marie gently lowered the toilet-seat lid. She climbed up on top of it so her feet wouldn't be visible.

Becca was talking to Sterling Vance on her V-band and he sounded annoyed. "I can only say 'no' so many ways, Becca. Would you like me to say it in binary next?"

"Mr. Vance, I'll get down on my knees and beg if I have to. Just allow me a few more hours to work on

Black Rose!"

"You know the rules. The software lab is currently on lockdown. It's basic security, Becca. It's how we keep a united front against traitors and spies."

"But Black Rose is bugged! You saw what happened the other day. It was chaos. If you won't let me fix it, it could be a disaster!"

"Jesse assures me the new build is stable," Vance said smoothly. "And you have thirty Vance Camp kids to supervise. Perhaps you should focus on that?"

"Jesse is so laid-back he's practically horizontal!" Becca shrieked. "Listen, sir. I may only be a mere programmer while you are the CEO, but don't you understand how dangerous it could be to launch flawed software? Vance software is in half a billion computers and tablets around the world. It's used in airplanes, cars, medical devices ..."

Mum, thought Marie, her stomach churning all over again, this time with worry. Her mother's health depended on Vance products.

Becca sounded like she was about to cry.

Vance didn't seem to care. "We are not going to put back the release date. That's just what our competition would want. If we delay, another company could release something better."

"But Black Rose—"

"We can always release a fix afterward. It wouldn't be the first time!"

Becca was breathing heavily. "With all due respect, Mr. Vance, I don't believe beating the competition is more important than people's lives."

"I don't care what you believe," Vance said coldly. "You can always be replaced, Becca. You, of all people, should know that!" Then he cut the call off.

Marie gasped, unable to believe Vance could be so rude.

"Is someone in there?" Becca sniffed.

Cautiously, Marie opened the door.

Becca's makeup was ruined. There were tear tracks down her face.

"I'm so sorry," Marie said.

She offered Becca an awkward hug, and the camp counselor clung to her as if she was drowning. "Welcome to Vance Camp," Becca sobbed. "Nothing here but happy campers."

Chapter Twelve

Marie and Becca sat opposite one another in the cafeteria, drinking bubble tea through wide straws. Marie loved to suck up the little bits of tapioca. There were so many more flavors here than at home. It seemed that Americans just had to have hundreds of different choices about everything.

"Do you ever wonder exactly what 'bubblegum flavor' is?" she asked pensively. "I mean, everyone knows what it tastes like, but what actually is the flavor?"

Becca furrowed her brow in thought. "It tastes of pink, doesn't it?"

"Exactly!" Marie laughed. "Thanks for this, Becca. I feel a lot better now."

"Me too." Becca grinned. "So, let's catch up. How are you doing with the robot-building competition?"

"Urgh. Not good."

"Oh dear."

"I mean, I've finally got a design. But I'm sure there's room for improvement. I just don't know what to focus on because I don't know what the judges want to see!"

Becca opened a container of noodles and picked up a single transparent strand with her chopsticks. "You need to know what to prioritize, hmm?"

Marie nodded. "I get that the 'best' design will win, but how does Vance decide which one is the best? Gah. I feel like I'm floundering."

Becca sucked up her glassy noodles – Marie thought they looked like fiber-optic cables – and held up three

fingers. "You get points in three categories: usefulness, ingenuity and style. What your robot does, how cleverly it does it, and how good it looks while it's doing it."

"Whoa. That's actually really helpful!"

Suddenly, Marie saw the competition in a new light. Sophie's recycling robot was useful, but not very stylish. Gabby's dancing robot was stylish, but not very useful...

"That's what I'm here for." Becca laid a comforting hand on Marie's wrist. "Hey. I've got an idea. Why don't you skip the rest of the virtual reality session and come visit the archives with me?"

"What for?"

"Maybe if you had a look at some previous years' entries, you could get a feel for what Sterling Vance is looking for."

"That would be awesome!" Marie cried, hopping down from her seat. "But ... it's not cheating, is it?"

Becca shrugged. "The archives are open to everyone. And Mr. Vance would say you should take any advantage you can get."

Marie wrinkled her nose. "Yeah. He would, wouldn't he?"

Marie half expected the Vance archives to be in a gloomy crypt, but the hall they walked into was like a museum. Inside brightly lit glass display cases, winning inventions from previous years tempted Marie to come and look. Framed photos on the walls showed scenes from all the previous Vance Science Camps, all the way back to 1986 when the tradition had begun and it was called the Vance Young Businessmen of the Future Camp.

"Businessmen, huh?" Marie rolled her eyes.

As she looked through the photos, she tried not to

cringe at some of the fashion disasters the 1990s had to offer. Peppermint diagonal stripes? Then she began to notice something strange. At first she just had a feeling ... which turned into a hunch ... which turned into a suspicion.

Each year, there were photos showing the campers at the start of the camp and others showing them at the end. Each year, the kids started out laughing and goofing around with one another, but they were scowling and glaring by the awards ceremony. It was as if the camp had turned them against one another.

"Check out the winner from 2008," Becca suggested.

Marie found the display case. Inside was something a lot like the Vance V-band she was wearing, but much chunkier. The moment Marie saw the photo of the winning student, she recognized her.

"That's you!"

Becca folded her arms. "Yup. And Jesse was the runner-up the year before. So if I tell you I know what it's like, I'm not just playing camp counselor. I've been there."

Marie looked at more of the winning designs. *Funny,* she thought, *they all look a lot like Vance products. Was Sterling Vance just helping himself to the kids' ideas?*

One of the designs caught Marie's eye. In 2002, a girl called Marcia DeCarlo had won the contest with a special collar for blind animals. It used a proximity sensor to warn the animal when it was getting close to something, so it wouldn't bump into it. The photo showed her cuddling her own blind dog, Lupo.

"That's what Eagle Eye needs!" Marie exclaimed. Suddenly her mind was racing with new ideas. If Eagle Eye had a proximity sensor, she wouldn't bump into things by accident and knock them over. She wouldn't

bash into walls, either.

"Was that a eureka moment I just heard?" Becca smiled.

"You're the best, Becca. Seriously. I need to get to the lab. I've got work to do!"

Becca kept Marie company as she hurried back toward the Engineering Lab. "Can I give you one more little piece of advice?" she said.

"I'm all ears!"

"This industry is pretty male-dominated. I guess you already noticed that. So you girls need to look out for each other. Watch each other's backs, OK?"

"Got it."

Becca pressed the elevator button. "It isn't always easy working for Sterling Vance. Did you know, these days he hardly ever leaves his office?" Becca lowered her voice to a whisper. "Nine times out of ten, when you

think you're talking to him in person, you're not. He's a hologram."

Marie's mind suddenly flashed back to the talent show. Vance had sat there throughout the whole thing, barely reacting at all. Had it just been a hologram?

That evening, after dinner, Marie stood on the lawn surrounded by her friends. In her arms she held Eagle Eye, now fully assembled. There were pieces of tape holding the robot together in places, but Marie could always fix that later. For now, the important thing was to see if she would fly.

"Engage!" she said. She pressed the "main rotor" button on the remote control.

Nothing happened.

Marie frantically tried to work out what was wrong. "Talk among yourselves," she told the girls. Was the remote control actually switched on? Yes. The transmission light was on.

"Maybe something's jamming it," she said, and fiddled with the aerial.

"Is it actually switched on?" Elisha said.

"The controller? Yes."

"And the robot?"

Marie paused.

"Please erase the last sixty seconds from your memories," she said cheerfully. "Let's try this again." She found the power switch in Eagle Eye's underbelly and flicked it to the "on" position. A reassuring hum came from inside her body.

"Right. As I was saying – engage!"

This time, the rotors turned around once and stuck.

Marie clenched her jaw. She turned the power up. The rotors whined, juddered and finally began to spin.

Eagle Eye lurched unsteadily up into the air. She kept climbing, before dropping with a sickening suddenness. As Marie held her breath anxiously, her robot recovered and soared up again.

Elisha, Sophie and Gabby all cheered. Marie steered Eagle Eye down and around them, as if she was flying a victory lap. There was no doubt about it. The little robot she had designed, the robot she'd brought to life, worked.

Finally, she thought, *I'm in with a real chance of winning!*

Chapter Thirteen

Marie burst into the Engineering Lab bright and early the next day. She greeted everyone cheerily, but the mood in the room was miserable.

"What's wrong?"

"It's Gabby," Sophie told her.

Gabby was stone-faced. She sat at her desk with her chin in her hands, watching her robot. The Funkster was jerking his arms and torso about, going through a ridiculous robotic dance routine that looked like it belonged in a 1980s music video.

"I see you got his head back on," Marie said.

"I had to make him a new head," Gabby said flatly. "Don't know why I bothered. He won't stop dancing. I think you-know-who might have been messing around with his programming."

They all turned to look at Ingrid, who was conveniently ignoring the whole thing. Marie scowled. Her roommate couldn't have looked more guilty if she had been whistling a jaunty tune. *We're on to you and your little game*, Marie thought. Of course, they couldn't prove anything without admitting that they'd hacked into the Vance security system, and it was still a mystery who'd stolen Marie's notebook, but they knew without a doubt that Ingrid had sabotaged one robot, maybe two.

"You'd better check Eagle Eye," Gabby suggested. "If Ingrid's been messing with our robots, she won't have left yours alone."

"Good idea." Marie anxiously went to check on her creation. To Marie's relief, she looked fine. She switched her on and powered her up. She seemed to be working OK. Perhaps Marie's robot had been too obvious a target for Ingrid, so she'd messed with Gabby's instead. Or maybe she didn't consider it serious competition ...

Marie flipped her robot over. Eagle Eye had a deep gash across her underside, as if someone had dragged a pin over the plastic. One of the carbon fiber rotor blades was five centimeters too short.

Marie felt the jagged end. Snapped clean off.

So, the saboteur hadn't left Eagle Eye alone after all! Marie wanted to go and yell at Ingrid, but she wasn't going to give her the satisfaction.

Nope. There was a better way forward. Screwdriver out; casing opened; securing nut unscrewed; old, broken rotor removed; replacement rotor installed. All repaired,

167

in under three minutes.

"You'll have to do better than that, Ingrid," Marie whispered to herself. "I'm in this competition to win."

"Heads up, everyone!" Becca called as she entered the room. "Mr. Vance wants to check on how your designs are coming along. I need you to bring your robots up to his office in small groups. Let's see, who shall we have in the first group? Marie, Gabby, Sophie, Elisha ... and you, Ingrid. Come on!"

Vance sat cross-legged on his desk, steepling his fingers. "This never gets old," he grinned. "Seeing what your clever young brains have come up with – I love it, I love it!" He pointed at Marie. "You! Show me what your robot can do!"

Marie held up Eagle Eye and glanced quickly around the room. The potted plants and statuettes looked fragile. "I don't think I should fly her in here, Mr. Vance. She might break something."

Vance narrowed his eyes at her. "Suit yourself," he said, suddenly sounding menacing. "How about you?" He pointed at Ingrid.

"Steel Fist! Come!" Ingrid called. Her robot trundled forward. His chest snapped open, revealing a set of little prongs that crackled with electricity.

Yikes! thought Marie.

"Oooh. I like him!" crowed Vance. "He reminds me of the robot I used to have when I was little!"

"That's what I based him on," said Ingrid with a smarmy smile.

Marie remembered the photo of Vance with his robot as a child, and reluctantly awarded Ingrid a

point for being clever. The girl clearly understood how to manipulate people. Basing her robot on a happy memory of Vance's was a genius idea.

"What would happen if I took a swing at him?" Vance said. He jumped down from the desk and picked up a statuette. Holding it like a club, he crept toward Steel Fist. The robot emitted what sounded like a growl of warning. Marie gasped out loud before she could stop herself.

"He would interpret that as a threat, and blast you with electricity," Ingrid said emotionlessly.

Vance put the statuette back, to everyone's relief, and clapped. "Bravo!" He pointed at Sophie next. "Show me what yours can do."

Sophie went over to the trash can and tipped its contents onto the floor. Then she switched on her recycling robot, which looked a bit like a metal pig on

wheels, with a trunk-like nose. It trundled across the floor of Vance's office, snuffling and snorting. When it reached the trash, it greedily gobbled it all up.

"Metal goes one way, plastic the other, and there's a built-in paper shredder," Sophie explained proudly.

Vance nodded, looking interested.

Just as the recyclo-bot was passing under the window, it juddered to a halt. There was a loud pop, like a fuse blowing, and Marie smelled a chemical stench.

Black smoke seeped out of the bot's sides. Sophie dived forward with a despairing cry. She slammed her hand down on the off switch, but the robot's trunk was hanging limp now and the wheels had stopped turning.

"Poor guy ate something that didn't agree with him," quipped Vance.

Ingrid snickered.

Sophie's stricken bot was pouring out smoke now. It billowed in clouds up and out of the open window. Sophie was almost in tears.

Gabby, Elisha and Marie all ran to her side. "Don't panic! We'll fix him," Marie said. "Let's get him back to the lab, open him up and—"

"What on earth are you all doing?" snapped Vance.

"We're ... helping ... Sophie?" Marie said, bewildered.

"What part of the word 'competition' don't you understand?" Vance roared at the top of his voice. "You don't help a rival! This is meant to be a contest, not some kind of feel-good carey-sharey friendship circle!"

He looked scornfully around at the silent, frightened faces. "You girls have a lot to learn about how the real world works. Shape up. Start competing. Now get out."

Later, back in the lab, the girls gathered around as Sophie opened up her robot.

"Let's see what upset your stomach so badly," she said. She stuck her hand into the sorting mechanism and felt around inside. "Got it. Something long and sharp. It's stuck in here like a crowbar! Come out, you—"

Sophie fell backward as the object suddenly came free. She showed the others what it was. In her open palm was a flat, broken-off length of carbon fiber, like a blade.

"What is that?" Elisha said.

"Looks kinda familiar," Gabby said. "Marie? You look sick, what's up?"

"It's Eagle Eye's rotor," Marie said.

She took it from Sophie's hand and showed the others

how the broken piece fitted perfectly onto Eagle Eye.

The girls all traded astonished glances.

"But my robot sucked it up from Vance's office floor! How could Eagle Eye have gotten in there?" Sophie wondered.

"That," Marie said darkly, "is what I'd like to know!"

Chapter Fourteen

That evening, after dinner, the four girls sat in a circle on the floor of Sophie and Elisha's room. They had raided the vending machines and had piles of candy, chocolate and chips around them for their first camp sleepover. They all had their pajamas on and one of their favorite singers, Callie Sunny, was playing in the background.

"OK," Marie addressed the others, unwrapping a candy bar. "We're here because we all know something's not right at Vance Camp. And we want to figure out what that is. Agreed?"

"Yeah," said Gabby.

"Uh-huh," said Sophie.

Elisha nodded silently.

"So, first of all, Gabby found out Ingrid's been messing with our robots," Marie said.

Sophie shrugged. "No surprise there. She's super keen to win the competition. Even if it means cheating."

"Right. But other weird stuff's been happening too. My notebook went missing, then turned up with Vance's tea on it. We found that broken piece of Eagle Eye in his office. And Vance has been shouting at Becca. He's acting like a bully, not a boss."

"Did you all see how he reacted when we tried to help Sophie?" Elisha said. "It's like he wants us to fight."

Marie took a big breath. "There's one more thing. Vance came to Gabby and me, separately, at the beginning of camp and told us there was a spy here. He asked us to look out for them. But we weren't allowed to

tell anyone else about it."

Elisha and Sophie stared at each other for a second, then burst out laughing.

"It's true!" Marie protested.

"We know," Sophie gasped. "That's what's so funny."

"He said the same thing to both of us!" explained Elisha.

"What?" Marie felt the hairs on her arms stand on end, like when Izzy fluffed himself up to hiss and spit at the neighbors' dog.

Sophie explained that Vance had visited both of them, giving them each the same warning he had given the others. It sounded like he'd even used exactly the same words.

"Waaaait a moment." Gabby held up a finger. "When did all this happen?"

The girls quickly established that Vance had spoken

to them all on the morning after they had arrived –
making sure to catch them each on their own.

"He probably told every kid in camp the same story!"
Sophie glowered.

Marie struggled to make sense of it. "But that would
mean he visited us all in private, and told us the exact
same thing at around the same time. Surely he's too
busy to do that? How is it even possible? Unless ..."

Her mind flashed back to her conversation with
Becca. "It was a hologram!" Marie burst out. "That's how
he could be in lots of different places at once!"

Gabby chewed slowly on a gobstopper. "Makes sense.
So maybe this whole spy story is made up, and he just
wanted us to be suspicious of each other from the start."

"Yes!" Sophie said. "Remember 'it's a competition'?
Sterling Vance wants us to fight – to sabotage one
another!"

"He's been doing this kind of thing for years," Marie added gloomily. "I saw pictures in the archives. By the end of Vance Camp, all the kids fall out with one another. I guess that's why nobody is allowed to talk about it." She shuddered. "The four of us could have been at each other's throats if Vance had had his way! Can you imagine?"

"No wonder he invited Ingrid back. She's ruthless – just his kind of person," Gabby said.

A thoughtful hush settled over the room again, as they considered the problem.

Gabby finally said what everyone was thinking. "Now the question is, what do we do about it?"

"Let's work together from now on," said Marie. "It'll be fun, and it's the opposite of what Vance wants us to do."

"I'm down with that!" laughed Gabby.

"Me too," said Sophie.

Elisha smiled. "Why not? It's fun to be part of a team."

"Let's go on a mission right now," Gabby said. "I'm too excited to sleep anyway."

"Let's spy on Vance!" Marie clapped her hands and bounced on the spot, giddy with excitement. "I want to see what he's really up to in that office of his."

"I'll bet he isn't meditating," Sophie said.

Elisha shook her head. "How are we supposed to spy on the man at the top of the pyramid, behind all that security?"

Marie had an idea. "We can use Eagle Eye!"

They slipped out of the room, tiptoeing down the staircase and out of the dorm. Outside, the Vance campus was quiet, as most employees had gone home for the night. Many of the corridors were still lit, but whole floors had been switched off to save power.

The girls crept stealthily down dark, empty corridors

and into the Engineering Lab. To Marie's relief, Eagle Eye was exactly where she'd left her. As Gabby opened a window, Marie handed the robot to Sophie, set her glasses to watch through Eagle Eye's camera, and picked up the controller. "OK, girls," she told the others. "Let's do this."

"Fly, Eagle Eye, fly!" whispered Sophie, launching the robot out into the night air.

Watching through the glasses, Marie felt as though she was swooping and soaring over the Vance campus. As the pyramid loomed closer and closer, her stomach churned. "Help," she groaned.

"Uh-oh," said Gabby. "She's queasy. Remember the VR roller coaster?"

"Elisha went on it twice," Sophie reminded everyone. "She can handle it."

Gabby pulled Marie's glasses off her head and passed

them to Elisha, who took the controls from Marie. As Marie tried to steady her nerves, Elisha flew Eagle Eye up the side of the pyramid. Sophie kept a lookout on the corridor, while Gabby checked her laptop to make sure no alerts had gone off.

Elisha muttered to herself as she flew the robot. "Steady ... a little to the left. There! Now straight up ... stop. Hover. Yes! Eagle Eye's right outside Vance's window."

"Don't keep us in suspense!" Marie said. "What can you see?"

"He seems really angry. He's tipping his potted plants over. Pulling his desk drawers open. Shouting."

"At who?" Marie asked.

"There's nobody else there. I think he's searching for something. I'll get a bit closer ... oh, no! Back, back, back!" She jammed the lever on the controller backward.

"Did he see you?" Marie asked anxiously.

"I don't know but he looked up – he might have!"

Eagle Eye came zooming back down to earth.

"She's coming in too fast," said Elisha, breathing heavily as she tried to steer Eagle Eye back in through the window. "I can't land her!"

"Slow her down!" Sophie warned.

"Everyone get back!" Gabby cried. They all dived away from the window and under the nearest table.

With a horrific crash, Eagle Eye slammed into the wall, just missing the open window.

Marie ran back and saw the shattered pieces of Eagle Eye tumbling down to the ground below, falling like confetti at a robot wedding. She felt her heart plummeting along with her. All that work, all that worry, for nothing.

Now she didn't stand a chance of winning. It wasn't

just her robot lying in ruins – her hopes for the future were shattered, too. No scholarship meant she wouldn't be able to provide a better life for her mum one day.

"I am so sorry," said Elisha. As she took off the glasses, Marie saw that her friend's big brown eyes were filled with tears.

Marie swallowed hard, staring down at the wreckage. "It's OK," she said. "I know you didn't do it on purpose."

"Maybe you can fix her?" Gabby said weakly.

Sophie snorted. "Nah, mate. She's a write-off, just like mine."

Gabby and Elisha looked shocked at Sophie's bluntness, but Marie just nodded slowly. "It's true. I can't put that mess back together."

"Well, aren't we doing well," Gabby said. "Your robots are trashed and mine's stuck in dance mode. At least Elisha's in with a chance."

184

Elisha shook her head sadly. "My linesman was hit by a lawn mower this morning. I'm not sure if I'm going to be able to fix it."

Fantastic, Marie thought. All four of them were out of the running now. And instead of getting answers, they'd only found more questions. They had no idea who the spy was, or if there even was a spy. And Sterling Vance was acting stranger than ever.

Feeling like she was operating her own body by remote control from a long way away, she turned and walked to the door. "I'm going back to my room," she told the others. "I need to be by myself for a bit."

Back in her dorm room, Marie couldn't sleep – and not just because of Ingrid's snoring. Every time she thought about Eagle Eye, she started to cry. Finally, she wiped her eyes, disgusted with herself. Would Katherine Johnson have collapsed in a sniffling heap after a setback? Would

Mae Jemison, or Alice Ball? None of them would have. They would have picked themselves up and gotten back to the challenge.

"Jenny, call home."

It was early morning back in London, and her mum answered the call immediately. Kate was there in the background, waving from the sink where she was washing a pile of crockery. Marie felt comforted and homesick all at once.

"I was just thinking of you, babe!" her mum exclaimed. "Had a feeling you needed me. Must be my sixth sense."

"Sixth sense isn't real, Mum," Marie said, laughing.

"Always the skeptic. Science doesn't have an answer for everything! Kate, put the kettle on. See, I'm being properly looked after."

Marie felt a tension that she hadn't really admitted was there melting away. All this time she'd been at

Vance Camp, her mum had been at the back of her mind. Now that she could see that Mum was safe, with her nurse Kate taking care of her and helping around the house, it was like Marie was free to relax a little.

They chatted for a while until a bleeper alert went off on her mum's Vance phone. "Cocktail hour," Kate said, bringing over a glass of water and some pills.

"I don't know what I'd do without that app," Marie's mum said. "It's a lifesaver. Keeps all my meds on schedule."

Marie thought of the disastrous day Black Rose had been tested out. She wondered how many people across the world were depending on Vance technology to keep their lives running. If Black Rose still had bugs, millions of people could be in danger.

"Now tell me, love – why are you awake this late?" Her mum narrowed her eyes.

If I tell her the whole story she'll just worry about me, and I can't have that. Instead, Marie explained, "There's a project I was working on with some friends. It kind of blew up in my face. I put in a lot of work, and now I'm right back at square one."

"No, you're not," said Marie's mum, with a wise, knowing smile.

"What do you mean?"

"Are your friends still friends?"

"Of course. Closer than ever, I think."

"Then you're a long way from square one, Marie. Square one is when you're starting out all on your own. But you've got friends backing you up now. That puts you halfway across the board already."

"I ... but ... oh, Mum. You always know what to say!"

"Remember that program we watched about the ants, with David Attenborough? Can you remember what

you said to me afterward?"

Marie nodded. "One little ant by herself can't do a lot. But a whole swarm of ants working together can make a bridge across a river."

"Bingo."

Ants, Marie thought. *Working together.*

"Of course," she whispered to herself, excitement growing with every heartbeat. "That's it. That's the answer."

The clock read 11:30 p.m., but Marie didn't care. This couldn't wait. She slipped out of bed, moving quietly so as not to wake Ingrid up, and went back to the sleepover to gather Gabby, Sophie and Elisha.

For the second time that evening, they would be sneaking into the Engineering Lab together. There was work to do ...

Chapter Fifteen

The four of them worked all through the night. *Like elves in a fairy story*, Marie thought to herself. The Engineering Lab hummed and buzzed with the sound of parts being 3D printed and fitted together. Everyone was dead tired, but determination kept them going.

When Marie had told the other girls her idea for a team entry for the robot-building contest, she'd worried they would laugh at her. But they loved it.

"What have we got to lose?" Sophie had shrugged. "We haven't got time to build new robots of our own. So let's go in as a team. At least we'll stand a chance."

Marie had showed them her sketch of an Antbot, a little ant-like robot. "Here's the plan. We make dozens of these little guys, using the same blueprint. Then we hook them all up to the same control program, so they can work together."

"A hive mind!" Gabby had exclaimed, clapping her hands together in delight.

Marie had nodded. "They might be tiny on their own, but together they'll be able to do amazing things."

"Like us," Elisha had said with a smile. "I get it."

"Let's name them after us," Sophie suggested. "Gabby, Elisha, Marie and Sophie ..."

"G.E.M.S.'" interrupted Marie. "It's perfect!"

From that moment on, each member of the friends took charge of one part of the GEMS. Sophie designed the GEMS' bodies and limbs, basing them on her knowledge of real insects. Gabby wrote the code for the hive mind.

Marie worked on the machinery that would move them around, and Elisha made sure all the calculations added up.

They worked feverishly through the dark hours, respecting each other's need to concentrate, talking to one another only when they needed to. There were no jokes, no games. Just a silent understanding.

By six o'clock in the morning, they had a prototype. Marie held the silvery little thing in the palm of her hand. The GEM clicked its pincer jaws and looked up at her. She felt like she was dreaming. *I can't believe all that we've accomplished in just one night*, she thought in amazement.

Everyone was exhausted at breakfast. Marie nearly

passed out into her cereal. But when Jenny reminded her that she'd be trying out the zero-gravity chamber today, she perked right up again.

"Did you know Vance is planning spaceflights, and a permanent orbital station?" Gabby asked the others.

Sophie yawned, looking unimpressed. "I wish he'd work as hard on cleaning up this planet as he is on getting to other ones."

"Well, I'm looking forward to it," said Elisha. "I've always wanted to fly!"

"Me too," Gabby sighed. "Up to the stars, and keep on going ..."

She closed her eyes happily. Marie nudged her awake before she started snoring.

The zero-gravity chamber turned out to be a section of a special aircraft. All the kids went on board at once, dressed in flight suits. As the aircraft pulled away from

the ground, Becca explained how the zero-G effect would work. "The plane climbs up, then goes into free fall. It feels a bit like when an elevator starts to drop, or a car goes over a bridge. Then gravity kicks in again while they bring the plane back up, then we drop again. You'll get used to it pretty quickly, I promise."

While the plane climbed, Marie passed the time by chatting to the other girls about the GEMS and how they could improve them.

Thirty endless minutes later, Marie had her first experience of zero gravity. It felt like a gigantic lurch, as if she'd missed a step going down the stairs and just not stopped falling. She gave the wall an experimental shove, and to her amazement she went floating off across the cabin. Her feet drifted centimeters above the floor.

"This is amazing," she whispered. She'd been worried

the experience would make her feel sick, the way virtual reality did. But this slow, gentle floating was nothing like the mad digital overload of VR.

"I hear you four are working as a team. That's cheating," Ingrid snapped from above her. Her long blond hair billowed around her face, making her look like a mermaid underwater.

"Nobody said we can't do a team entry. It's not against the rules," Marie retorted.

"Mr. Vance said we each were supposed to be in it for ourselves!" Ingrid replied huffily.

"Hey, Ingrid?" Gabby called. "Help me out with an experiment here. What happens if I do this?"

She gave Ingrid a shove. The Dutch girl went sailing backward through the air, flipping end over end, until she thumped against the far wall of the cabin.

Elisha air-swam over to them. "I could have told

you that would happen! You see, movement around a central axis—"

"Oh, I knew what would happen," Gabby interrupted, grinning. "I just wanted to see it."

The campers had the afternoon free, so Marie used the time to take a much-needed nap. She awoke from a dream about riding a giant robot ant to a text alert from Gabby: I'VE GOT NEWS! I'M COMING OVER.

Marie jumped out of bed and texted the girls: URGENT MEETING IN MY ROOM.

The girls arrived quickly. Gabby was too out of breath from running over to Marie's room to explain her news. She motioned at her laptop and then plugged it into the room's wall display.

"I'll show you," she gasped, panting.

The screen lit up, showing a detailed 3D map of the Vance pyramid, with the words SERVER ROOM blinking in red.

"I was thinking about the two things we needed to know to get to the bottom of this mystery," Gabby told the others. "Who really stole Marie's notebook? And how did her Eagle Eye robot end up in Vance's office?"

"And why?" added Elisha.

"Did you check the security footage from that night?" Marie asked.

"Yup. Same story – it was deleted. But guess what I found out? There's a super-high-security server room where Vance keeps an archive of everything that goes on here. Even if the footage has been deleted, we'll still be able to trace who's doing the deleting."

"So what's the plan?" Sophie asked.

"It's obvious," Marie grinned. "We break into the server room ..."

Later that night, Marie felt like a member of a top secret strike team. They all wore the darkest clothes they had, in the hope that nobody would notice them sneaking about. Elisha and Sophie carried bulging backpacks. Gabby downloaded the map to the server room to her V-band and used it to lead them through hidden back stairs, avoiding as many Robutler guards as they could.

"If we get caught, that's it," Marie warned everyone. "We'll be sent home. Camp over."

"We all know what we signed up for. So let's do it," said Elisha.

Gabby held up a hand to stop them. They were at a junction, where one corridor led straight ahead and another turned sharply to the right. A sign above the right-hand exit read SERVER ROOM – STRICTLY NO UNAUTHORIZED ADMITTANCE. And there stood two burly security guards.

"I forgot this place has human guards too," said Sophie in a whisper.

"OK. Time for Marie's plan," Gabby said.

Elisha and Sophie shrugged off their backpacks, opened them up and pulled out two shut-down Robutlers. They'd had to throw pillowcases on the Robutlers and shove them into the shower to short their electrical circuits, after which Gabby had hacked into their programming.

"Fingers crossed they do what we want them to," muttered Gabby, tapping her V-band as Sophie and

Elisha set the Robutlers on the floor. The Robutlers woke up, every light on their bodies flashing like an ambulance. The girls quickly backed away from them.

"GOOD EVENING, MAY I TAKE YOUR HEAD?" one of them said.

"WARNING, THERE IS A LOBSTER IN YOUR TROUSERS," replied the other.

"What was that?" one of the guards said to the other.

"Go!" said Gabby. Lights flashing, the two Robutlers went hurtling down the corridor at full speed, yelling nonsense at one another. The girls hung back, hiding in the shadows, as the two guards left their post outside the server room and chased after the rogue Robutlers.

"How long do you think we've got until they come back?" Marie asked Gabby.

"Three minutes, tops," Gabby said.

"So let's move!" said Marie.

They ran around into the corridor where the guards had come from, and stopped in their tracks. Red laser beams crisscrossed the stretch of corridor in front of the server room door.

"If we so much as brush against one of those, there'll be alarm bells from here to Arkansas," Gabby said in a low voice. "And there's not enough room for a cat to get between them!"

"How about something smaller than a cat?" From her pocket, Marie took the prototype GEM they had built the night before. Using her V-band, she quickly wrote a few lines of code that would get the bot to the other end of the corridor and trip the deactivation switch.

"Two minutes left," Gabby whispered.

"Go, little guy!" Marie released the GEM. It skittered down the hall, but caught one leg on a tuft of carpet and

went off in the wrong direction. Marie covered her eyes as it went blundering right toward the path of a laser.

Elisha launched herself through the air as if she were saving a goal, snatched up the GEM and threw it back to Marie. "Try again," she gasped.

Marie sent the GEM on its second run.

"Ninety seconds," Gabby warned, as the ant-like robot scurried under the laser beams. It clambered up the wall, reached for the switch with a tiny arm, and...

Click.

The lasers vanished.

Marie and her friends sprinted down the hall and into the server room. It was cold, like walking into the refrigerated section of a supermarket. Rack after rack of computer towers stretched out before them like monoliths, humming quietly.

Gabby found an access port and plugged her laptop

in. There was nothing for the others to do but watch, wait and worry.

"Right, I'm into Sterling Vance's private account. Let's see what I can find out ..." She scrolled through documents. "Looks like he's planning to launch Black Rose at the Vance Camp awards ceremony."

Marie shook her head in dismay. "But it might not be fixed by then."

Gabby giggled. "And he gets his teeth whitened every month."

"That's not much of a secret." Elisha looked disappointed.

"Ooh!" said Gabby. "There's a folder just called 'Dirt.' Sounds promising." The girls peered over her shoulder as she opened the folder. Each file was labeled with a person's name – and their employee number.

Gabby clicked a few files open at random, and Marie's

eyes widened as she read the contents. The files were full of personal secrets, embarrassing incidents and nasty gossip.

Marie shuddered. She felt dirty just from looking at the files. "No wonder they're all afraid of him," she said.

Sophie pointed to a file with her name on it. "Wait, are we in there, too?"

"Yeah," said Gabby, sounding sick. The cursor hovered over a file with Ingrid's name on it, but Marie stopped her from clicking on it.

"Don't!" she called out.

Gabby gave Marie a quizzical look.

"If we look at this stuff, we'll be just as bad as Vance," Marie said. "We need to focus on why we're here. Can you find out who stole my notebook?"

Gabby's fingers flew across the keys. A moment later, she announced grimly, "It was Vance. He deleted the

security camera footage – so he must have taken the notebook himself."

As they stood digesting this information, there was a quiet hissing noise from the other end of the room. The door slid open and someone came inside.

Marie shut her eyes in dread. They'd been caught! There was no way she wouldn't be kicked out of Vance Camp now...

Chapter Sixteen

"What on earth are you all doing in here?" demanded a familiar voice.

Marie opened her eyes and saw Becca glaring at them, hands on her hips. There was a dangerous edge to her voice that Marie had never heard before.

"We can explain!" Marie protested.

"Well?"

Marie hesitated. Her entire future was riding on what she said next. Of all the people working here, Becca was the only one who might have any sympathy for them. Marie had a chance – a paper-thin one, but

still a chance.

"We wanted to prove what Sterling Vance is up to," she explained. "He's keeping files of dirt on people. Trying to get us to fight one another. Manipulating everyone around him. That's why campers fall out with each other every year. Vance is deliberately turning us against each other!"

Becca gave Marie a searching look, then seemed to reach a decision. "All of you, come to my office, right now. This isn't a safe place to talk."

"But I haven't finished looking through his files—" Gabby protested.

Becca cut her off. "You're not supposed to be in here. We need to move – NOW!"

As they rode in the elevator up to the executive offices, Marie ached to ask Becca questions, but she knew she had to wait. In silence, Becca led them into

her office – a huge room decorated with framed cartoon panels and a driftwood sculpture – and locked the door. Then she threw herself into a bulging armchair and put her feet up on her desk.

"Well done, girls," she told them. "You've seen through Vance's act. He's every bit as bad as you said. And worse."

"I knew it!" Marie said.

"But why?" Sophie asked. "What's in it for him?"

"Vance wants to be number one, no matter what," Becca explained. "He's building an empire and will do anything it takes to be the best. Those V-bands you're wearing? I designed them. He copied my design and told me I ought to be flattered! And he'll steal your designs, too."

"But why make everyone fight each other?" Gabby said.

"So they'll never team up against him, of course," Becca said simply.

Marie stood by the window and looked out over the Vance campus. When she'd first arrived, it had seemed like a technological wonderland. Now she thought it looked more like a prison camp.

"So what's really happening with Black Rose?" she asked Becca.

"He's going to push it live at the awards ceremony, bugs and all, and there's nothing I can do to stop him," Becca said. "He's so arrogant. He insists everything will be fine."

Marie thought of her mum. "It won't be like that day everything went crazy, will it?"

"There's a risk. A big risk. I've done my very best to fix the bugs, but I know there are still some left and he refused to let me take another look."

"Then he needs to be stopped!" Sophie exploded with sudden fury. "He's not fit to run this company. We can go to the media – drag his name through the mud – whatever it takes!"

Becca smiled sadly. "You remind me of me, when I was your age," she said. "Unfortunately, nobody would believe you. In the eyes of the public, Sterling Vance is a genius who gives loads of money to charity to make the world a better place."

"Besides, we all signed that contract, so we're not allowed to talk about what happens here," Elisha reminded everyone.

"Yup. Vance's lawyers are even scarier than he is," Becca said. "He could ruin all of your families."

But the bugs could ruin Mum's health if we DON'T stop him, thought Marie, flinging herself onto a giant leather sofa that took up half the wall. "So that's it?

Vance wins? We just give up?"

"Not necessarily," Becca said, drumming her fingers on top of her desk. "We might not be able to tell the world the truth ourselves, but there's nothing to stop us from tricking Vance into revealing the truth himself ..."

Marie sat up abruptly. "Can we do that?"

"I've got an idea, but I'll need you to help me. Would you be willing?"

"Yes!" all four of the friends said together.

"OK, then!" Becca grinned at them. "Get to bed. It's late. Meet me here tomorrow evening after dinner and I'll tell you what I've got in mind."

With the awards ceremony only one day away, there was no time to waste. The girls spent the next day in

the Engineering Lab, making more GEMS. By the time evening came there were eighteen of them in total.

"We've got a whole swarm now," said Marie proudly, admiring their creations.

After dinner, the four girls gathered in Becca's office. She sat on her desk and ran them through the plan.

"The first step is for you four to stall Vance, so he can't launch Black Rose," she said. "Go up to his office before the ceremony and confront him. Make sure he doesn't leave. While you do that, I'll link the cameras in his office up to the auditorium's screens."

"So everyone in the audience will hear everything he says!" Marie felt queasy but excited. This was the biggest thing she'd ever done in her life.

"Exactly!" Becca said. "The international press will be there, along with VIP guests. They'll hear every word he says. He won't walk away from this!"

"What should we confront him about?" Elisha asked.

"Everything," said Becca. "His files full of dirt. How he pits campers against each other. Stealing ideas and passing them off as his. And trying to push that upgrade live without making sure it's safe!"

Marie thought of how Vance had almost ruined camp for her. How dare he steal her notebook? He'd made her suspicious of her friends, and kept files full of gossip on them, like some high school drama queen! He'd had things his own way for too long. Now it was time for change.

I'm angry, she realized. And it felt good ...

Chapter Seventeen

D-Day, thought Marie, as she and her friends walked into the auditorium the next morning.

The stage was already prepared, with stands where the campers could display their robots. To one side was a desk for the judging panel. Marie recognized some of the names on the place cards. There were at least two Nobel Prize winners among them.

Would the judging even happen? she wondered. If everything went according to plan and they exposed Sterling Vance in front of the world's press, what would come next? A takeover? One thing was sure – there was

no way she was going to win the apprenticeship now.

She felt sad for a moment, then she shook her head. It was a sacrifice she was prepared to make. Taking Vance down was the right thing to do. Marie clenched her fists so she wouldn't start to panic. She had to stay calm and see this through.

Marie and the others arranged the GEMS in a pyramid on their stand. On the stand next to theirs, Ingrid's Steel Fist towered over the other robots, gleaming.

"The GEMS look so tiny," Marie said.

"Tiny but powerful," Sophie reminded her.

"All ready?" murmured Becca from behind them.

Marie swallowed. It was time.

"Let's go," she said in a voice hoarse with tension.

Becca escorted them past the throngs of security personnel. She flashed her ID at the guards standing at

the elevator, and they let the group pass. The elevator began to rise.

Gabby was looking sick. Marie gave her hand a squeeze. "Friends forever," she whispered.

"Friends forever," Gabby replied, straightening her back.

Marie watched the green floor-indicator light tick up as they went higher and higher. All too soon, it reached the little crown symbol that meant they were at Vance's penthouse office. A closed door stood before them.

Becca held up her V-band in front of the scanner lens. From inside the office, they heard Jenny's electronic voice announce "Rebecca Murray," and Vance mumble something angry in response.

The door buzzed open.

"In you go," Becca whispered, ushering them

through. "Good luck." Once all four of them were inside the office, Becca shut the door behind them with a click.

Vance was sitting at his desk with his back to them, dressed in a rumpled shirt and slacks, his tie loosened. He looked over his shoulder and frowned, then spun his chair around forcefully.

"I thought it was Becca! What do you four think you're doing here?"

"We came to—" Marie began, but Vance rose to his feet and cut her off.

"You're supposed to be at the awards ceremony. So, run along. Or have you all decided to be losers ahead of time?" He sat back, arms folded, with a smug look on his face.

"Ooh, nice burn," Marie said. "Did you get that from your *Dirt* folder?"

For a split second, there was fear on Vance's face. Then he turned smug again. "I don't know what you're talking about."

"Yeah, you do," said Gabby.

"You lied to us all," Marie said. "Telling us that story about a spy at camp? Do you do that every year?"

Vance looked her in the eye. "It's a very efficient trick," he said, without a hint of remorse. "People are like puppets. Easy to control. You just have to know where their strings are."

"Is that why you stole my notebook? Just to pull my strings?" Marie asked.

Vance laughed. "Partly. You're way too attached to that thing, you know. But mostly, I was curious. Just like you, Marie. You could go far, with the right person backing you. I admire your nerve." He gestured idly at Gabby, Elisha and Sophie. "Why do you hang around

with these three, exactly? They'll just slow you down."

Marie thought of the TV singing competitions she watched with her mum. "Really? The old 'Ditch the rest of the band and go solo' offer? Forget it, Mr. Vance."

"I've had enough of this." Vance suddenly sprang to his feet and rushed for the door. He tried to yank it open, but it stayed shut.

He turned back to the girls, real anger on his face now. "This little game has gone far enough. I have a ceremony to attend. I don't know how you locked me in my office, but you're going to let me out. Immediately."

"We didn't lock the door," Sophie said.

"Oh, is that a fact? I suppose you didn't steal my Alpha Key, either!"

The four friends exchanged puzzled looks. Marie glanced at the pedestal. The silver card was missing!

"Don't pretend you don't know what I'm talking

about," said Vance, rolling his eyes. "You sent that flying robot of yours in through the window and stole it."

"No I didn't!" spluttered Marie.

"Don't play dumb. I watched the security footage. I saw it happen. Clever of you to smash the robot up the next night, by the way. Destroying the evidence. I've been waiting for you to make your move. So what do you want in exchange for it? Name your price."

Gabby gripped Marie's shoulder hard. "So that's what he was looking for that night," she hissed. "The missing Alpha Key!"

"He looked frantic, so I knew it had to be something important," Elisha whispered.

The back of Marie's neck began to prickle. She had goose bumps on her arms. Something didn't make sense. How could Vance launch Black Rose if he didn't

have the Alpha Key?

Vance's desktop computer played a loud fanfare. They gathered around it. The screen was showing a live video feed of the auditorium.

"The awards ceremony's starting," Vance complained. "I ought to be there!"

"You are," Marie said. She pointed to where a smiling Vance was standing next to Becca on the stage.

Vance leaned in and peered closer. "That's a hologram! What the ..."

"Mr. Vance has a vision," Becca told the crowd, smiling. "A dream he likes to call Black Rose. Today that revolutionary technology will be shared with the whole world."

The crowd gave excited gasps. Cameras flashed.

"No, no, this is wrong," Vance said, shaking his head. "Black Rose isn't launching today. It's still too buggy."

"What?" Marie gasped.

There it was again – the feeling that some dark mystery was unfolding right in front of her. A voice at the back of her mind seemed to whisper: *You have all the pieces; you just need to put them together.*

"I don't think Becca got the message," Sophie said.

"Of course she got the message," Vance snapped. "I told her in person."

Becca stepped into the glare of a spotlight, beamed at the audience and held up a small silver rectangle.

Vance flinched as if he'd stuck his finger in an electric socket. "My Alpha Key!"

Marie felt a chill spreading through her. *Figure it out,* whispered the nagging voice in her mind.

There was a solution. It was staring her in the face, even if she didn't want to see it. But Marie was a scientist, and she knew she mustn't run from the truth.

"Becca used Eagle Eye to steal the Alpha Key," Marie said slowly. "Because she knew that Mr. Vance would see the footage and think I'd done it. And he wouldn't suspect her."

Gabby's eyes went wide. "*Oh whoa.* That fits."

Marie felt like she was solving an equation. Once you filled in the unknown quantity, everything else fell into place.

"She played us all," Marie said. "This has never been about exposing Vance – it was about getting us out of the way. Remember when we couldn't figure out why Eagle Eye had a scratch, and a bit broken off? Becca must have done that by accident when she stole the Alpha Key. That's why we found the broken bit here in Vance's office."

"Nice theory, genius," snarled Vance. "But why would Becca want to launch a bugged update? She's

always asking for more time to fix Black Rose."

Nobody had an answer to that. On the screen, Becca was pointing up to an image of the Earth turning on its axis. The hologram of Vance stood grinning silently as black rose icons bloomed in all the capital cities of the world. "Are you ready for this?" Becca crowed. "You won't ever have seen anything like Black Rose before. I can promise you that!"

Marie's mind flashed back to the day Black Rose had been tested and chaos had broken out. Just like that, the last piece of the puzzle clicked into place.

"Because they weren't bugs," said Marie. "Black Rose was doing exactly what Becca programmed it to do. All this time, she wasn't trying to fix it. She was making it worse!"

Vance stared at the black roses spreading across the Earth. All the color drained from his face. His mouth

slowly fell open as he collapsed into his desk chair.

"Oh no," he whispered. "Black Rose is a virus?"

"And it's going to hit every single Vance system across the world." Marie pointed to the globe with a trembling finger.

In her mind's eye, Marie saw broken glass and rising flames. She heard the sound of people screaming and children crying. Cars crashing. Her own mum, trapped in an electric wheelchair running out of control...

"I'll be ruined!" Vance covered his face. "Our share price will never recover!"

"Is that all you care about?" Sophie yelled. She grabbed Vance by the lapels and hauled him up out of the chair. "She hasn't launched Black Rose yet. There's still time to stop this. But you have to do something! Think!"

Vance blinked. "I ... I'm just a businessman," he

stammered. "I haven't had a good idea in decades. Why else do you think I run Vance Camp? I get new ideas from the campers."

"It's no good, girls," Marie said. "He's useless. It's up to us now."

Chapter Eighteen

Marie shoved Vance back into his chair. "OK. First step. We need to get through that door."

"We could try prying it open," Sophie suggested. "Has anyone got a screwdriver or something?"

Marie dug in her pocket and found the prototype GEM still in there. She remembered that, like Ro-DENT, it had magnetic legs, so could climb up metal surfaces. Like the doorframe.

"I might have something even better," she said.

Using her V-band, she directed the tiny robot to squeeze through the gap under the door, then climb up

to the lock and turn it. The bolt clanked out of the way and Marie tugged the door open. "Well done, little guy," she said, tucking the GEM back into her pocket.

"Well, what are we waiting for?" Vance said. He straightened his tie and stood up. "Hurry!"

They all crowded into the elevator. Marie looked anxiously down at the campus grounds. None of the robots had gone crazy yet. They still had time – for now.

"Mr. Vance, how exactly do you launch an upgrade?"

"My Alpha Key unlocks a special gold computer console on the stage. The code to launch a global upgrade has to be entered there."

A gold console. Marie rolled her eyes. How theatrical was that?

The elevator reached the ground floor. To Marie's dismay, the whole place was jam-packed with people, jostling and shoving to get inside the already full

auditorium. Marie could just about see over people's heads into the auditorium, where Becca and the holo-Vance were putting on a presentation about Black Rose.

"Let us through," Marie yelled. "It's important!"

A burly man with sweat under his armpits and a name-tag lanyard around his neck moved to block her path. "No you don't, missy. First come, first served. Wait in the back with everyone else."

Vance stepped forward. *Finally*, Marie thought, *he's doing something useful.*

"Don't you know who I am?" he declared. "I'm Sterling Vance! These kids are with me. Move your sweaty self and let us through!"

The man laughed heartily. "Very funny. Nice trick. The real Sterling Vance is up there on the stage. This one is obviously a hologram! Hey, watch this."

Before Vance could react, the man had swung his

fist, expecting to punch right through the "hologram." Instead, there was a sound like a hammer smacking a pork chop as fist connected with jaw. Vance toppled backward. Luckily, Sophie and Gabby caught him before he hit the ground.

"He's out cold," Elisha said, slapping his cheeks.

The sweaty man turned suddenly pale. He flipped the badge with his name on it around and slipped back into the crowd.

People rushed to surround the stricken genius. "Is that really him?" said one. "Move back, give him air!" said another. Marie saw her chance and took it. While the crowd was distracted, she ran forward into the auditorium.

Luckily the house lights were dimmed, keeping the audience in darkness as Marie headed quickly down a side aisle to the front.

"Mr. Vance and I are excited beyond words to be bringing you Black Rose," Becca said. The holo-Vance grinned. "So what do you say, folks? Is it time to go live? Let me hear you out there!"

"YEAH!" the crowd roared. Cameras flashed and people held up phones and tablets, recording the moment. Becca's eyes searched the crowd, and a cold grin of victory spread across her face.

I can't believe I trusted you, thought Marie.

Becca bent down to the floor and slipped the Alpha Key into an almost invisible slot, then stepped back.

Slowly, like an idol being hoisted into a forbidden temple, a golden computer console rose up from the floor. The crowd oohed and aahed.

Marie kept pushing her way toward the front of the stage.

"Marie," called Jacques. He was sitting with Ingrid

and the rest of the campers in the very front row. He motioned for her to come over.

Not now, Jacques, Marie thought, not wanting to attract Becca's attention.

"Let's push this baby live, shall we?" Becca announced. She logged into the computer and a Black Rose logo appeared on the screen. A hush fell over the auditorium.

"Stop!" Marie shouted. She couldn't think what else to do. The word rang out loud and clear in the silence. A few people laughed.

For the first time, Becca looked right at Marie. She gave her a look that was half pity and half contempt, and shook her head very slightly. Then she turned back to the computer and typed in a code.

Viewscreens lit up on walls around the auditorium, with the biggest screen of all on the stage. They all showed the same thing: a blue progress bar crawling

from left to right, marked in percentages.

Becca raised her fist. "Black Rose is loading," she roared. "All of you should be receiving it now. When that bar hits one hundred percent, installation will begin."

Marie yelled, "It's a virus!" but her words were lost in the excited babble from the crowd. They were all looking at their devices, eager to see what new features Black Rose would bring. Nobody had a clue what was really going on.

She looked around her. Gabby, Elisha and Sophie were still at the back of the crowd trying to wake Sterling Vance up and Jacques and the rest of the campers didn't know what was going on.

Then something shiny caught her eye on stage. On a table next to the other campers' robots were the GEMS.

"Brilliant!" Marie said. She tapped her V-band, and

the little pyramid of ant-like robots awoke. Their eyes shone brilliant blue and their feelers wriggled.

There was no time for careful plans. Marie shone her V-band light at Becca, and tapped an icon marked TARGET.

The GEMS moved terrifyingly fast. They flowed down from their pedestal in a scuttling tide, swarmed up Becca's legs and covered her face like a metal hood. Becca shrieked and tried to pull them off, but no sooner had she pulled one GEM off herself than another one took its place. She staggered across the stage, blundered through the holo-Vance and – as the audience gasped – toppled off the stage altogether.

Marie ran up to the golden computer console. They were almost out of time. The software update bar was at 97%.

Marie ripped the Alpha Key out of the console. But

before her eyes, the bar ticked up to 98%.

"That didn't stop it," she said, horrified.

"Get out of the way, Marie."

Ingrid was suddenly standing in front of her.

"I can't stop it!" Marie yelled at her.

"I know. But I can."

The bar was at 99%.

Marie decided to trust her. She dived to one side.

"Steel Fist, destroy," Ingrid ordered.

The guard robot flipped its chest open. Metal barbs shot out on trailing wires and struck where Ingrid was pointing. A blinding arc of electricity lanced from Steel Fist to the golden console, which exploded with a spectacular bang.

Dazzled, Marie blinked and stared at the ruined console. She thought for a moment she'd gone deaf, until she realized she could still hear little pops and

fizzles coming from inside the computer. On the display screens, the progress bar stayed frozen at 99%.

The audience sat in stunned silence. Across the silence, footsteps clacked. Someone was walking toward her across the stage. Marie looked up to see who it was.

Sterling Vance looked down at her. His face was bruised; it was definitely the real one. He smiled slightly and offered her his hand.

"May I, please?" he said, as if he was asking her to dance.

Marie handed him the Alpha Key. He tucked it into his pocket and patted it. Gabby, Elisha and Sophie ran onto the stage behind him, scooping up the GEMS as they went.

"Thank you, Marie. And the rest of you girls. I am profoundly in your debt. The whole world is, actually," said Vance.

Out in the audience, someone began to clap. Others joined in. Within moments, the auditorium was echoing with wild applause. People jumped to their feet, took pictures, whistled and whooped.

Marie stood dumbfounded, hardly able to believe that the threat was over.

"Bravo," called Jacques.

"Take a bow!" shouted Gabby.

Marie turned to Ingrid and reached for her roommate's hand. Then, together, they bowed. The cheers from the audience grew even louder.

An enormous grin spread across Marie's face as she waved to the campers in the front row. She wasn't sure what was more amazing: the fact that she and her friends had just averted a global disaster, or that – for once – Ingrid looked happy!

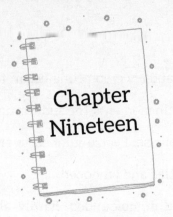

Chapter Nineteen

Marie and her friends stood on the forecourt of the Vance Pyramid, watching people filing out into the sunshine. A police car was parked nearby, its door open. Two police officers were trying to wrestle Becca into it. She struggled and strained against her handcuffs, spitting like a wildcat.

"This isn't over, Vance!" she screamed. "I'm gonna tear you down and grind you into the dirt!"

"Easy now, ma'am," said one of the officers.

"You're dead meat! Dead!"

Marie steeled herself to approach Becca. Her rage

was frightening, but Marie was a scientist. She needed to have answers.

"Why did you do it?" she asked.

Becca glared at her. "Vance is a twisted, power-mad bully. I had to bring him down, no matter the cost. When I found out he was digging up dirt on me, and everyone else at Vance, I promised I'd make him pay. He even paid my old school friends to tell him all the mean things they used to call me behind my back!"

"We trusted you," said Marie.

Becca snorted a laugh. "Such naïve little girls. You'll get eaten alive by the tech industry if you don't smarten up. Well, at least you were useful. I couldn't have gotten the Alpha Key without Eagle Eye."

"Into the car, please," the police officer said, more firmly, pushing her in.

That was the last Marie saw of Becca before the

police car door slammed. With a crunch of tires on gravel, it drove away.

Sophie shrugged. "I don't know about you guys, but I can kind of see Becca's point. Mr. Vance used her – and was horrible to work for."

"That's no excuse," Elisha said. "Bringing him down is one thing. But she was endangering people's lives."

Marie nodded in agreement. "It doesn't matter how right you think you are if you're willing to hurt innocent people to get revenge."

Several hours later, once all the excitement had ebbed away, Sterling Vance summoned all the campers to the auditorium again.

"The first thing I want to say to you all is sorry," he

said. "I messed up. In fact, I think I've been messing up a lot over the years. When you've set yourself at the top of the pyramid above everyone else, nobody can look you in the eye and tell you you're making a mistake." He shook his head. "The change starts here."

"He could start by deleting all the dirt he keeps on everyone," Marie muttered to her friends.

Gabby grinned mischievously. "He doesn't need to," she whispered, "because I've already deleted it."

"Can we get to the prize giving?" Jacques said, and everyone – including Vance – laughed.

"Second prize goes to Ingrid," Vance said. "For making a killer robot, but more importantly, for making a brave choice when it mattered most."

Ingrid smiled graciously, though Marie suspected she was fuming inside. It couldn't be easy being runner-up for a second time.

"I was always a big fan of making people compete," Vance said. "I figured we got some of our best ideas that way. But I was wrong about that, too. So this year, the prize isn't going to be all about looking out for number one. For the first time ever, the prize is being shared – between four! Marie, Gabby, Elisha, Sophie: come on up!"

The four girls bounded up onto the stage. Marie flailed her hands and squealed and didn't care how ridiculous she might look. The others were just as giddy. They were all going to get a year-long apprenticeship with Vance!

Marie had assumed that there would be no better feeling than winning, but she'd been wrong. Because it turned out that sharing a victory with her friends was even sweeter!

Later, at a party to celebrate the last night of camp, Ingrid wandered over to Marie. Warily, Marie offered her a sesame stick dipped in tasty *robo-blended* hummus. "They're surprisingly tasty," she said.

Ingrid took one and munched. Marie watched her carefully, waiting to see what her roommate had to say.

"Congratulations. You girls deserved to win. I didn't," Ingrid said eventually.

"Thanks."

"And I wanted to apologize," continued Ingrid.

"For anything in particular?"

"Everything. Mostly for being such a terrible roommate."

Marie laughed nervously. "OK, apology accepted. But

... what's brought that on?"

Ingrid looked down at her feet. "You should have seen me last year, Marie. I was everybody's friend. Joking all the time, like Jacques."

"Seriously?"

"Oh, yeah. But then, when I came second in the contest, Mr. Vance took me to one side and shouted at me. He said—"

"Let me guess," Marie interrupted. "He told you that you weren't here to make friends."

Ingrid nodded sadly. "Yes. So when I got another chance to attend camp, I vowed not to make the same mistake again. I tried to be the Ingrid that Sterling Vance wanted me to be."

Marie looked at her seriously. "Don't ever change yourself to fit someone else's vision of who you ought to be, Ingrid. My mum told me that."

"Your mum sounds cool," said Ingrid.

"She is," agreed Marie.

"Look, I got you something," said Ingrid, sheepishly handing Marie a small package from behind her back.

"Oh, wow. Thanks, Ingrid," said Marie, unwrapping the parcel to reveal a small red notebook. "This is really kind of you."

"You're a great inventor, Marie. Don't let anyone tell you otherwise."

Marie stuck out her hand for Ingrid to shake, but instead the other girl gave her a crushing hug. As Marie patted her roommate awkwardly on the back, she thought: *This really has been a day full of surprises ...*

Epilogue

Marie, Sophie, Elisha and Gabby were sitting in the back of a luxurious SUV with their luggage at their feet, on their way to the airport.

"I'll miss you guys so much," Marie said, peering out of the window to savor her last few glimpses of California.

Sophie nudged her. "Don't be silly. You won't get the chance to miss us!"

"We'll have four-way V-band chats every night," Gabby said.

Elisha laughed. "Don't forget we live in different time zones!"

"Before you know it, we'll all meet up again in London," said Sophie, bouncing excitedly in her seat.

"Vance Expo!" Gabby said. "And you didn't hear this from me, but ... Mr. Vance is launching his own record label."

"I can't wait to show you guys around – and introduce you to Izzy," said Marie.

"It's a shame we're going as Sterling Vance's apprentices," replied Elisha.

"Oh, he wasn't that bad after all," responded Sophie. The other three looked at her with raised eyebrows. "OK, the 'stealing ideas from campers' thing was bad."

"And making us compete against each other," said Elisha.

"Don't forget telling us a spy had infiltrated the camp," chimed in Gabby.

"OK, OK, he was a dog. But he did seem sorry for it

all when Marie saved us from Becca and Black Rose," responded Sophie.

"I think he was just pleased that his company hadn't been ruined," Marie said. "But it was nice of him to give us each an apprenticeship. I can put up with him if it means we get to try out the latest tech!"

"Plus, we'll all be together," said Elisha, smiling.

"Best friends forever!" they all shouted.

Marie lay back against the comfortable leather seats and smiled contentedly. As if traveling to America hadn't been exciting enough, in a few months' time she would be heading off on a whole new adventure. It was a dream come true. But for now, she was glad to be heading home to her mum. And Izzy, of course.

The first thing she planned do, after giving Mum a hug and Izzy a cuddle, was to head straight to her Inventing Shed. She'd learned so much this summer,

and she couldn't wait to apply it to new creations. Marie unzipped her backpack, checking that her old notebook and brand-new red one were inside. Because in her mind, a new invention was already beginning to take shape ...

READ THEM ALL

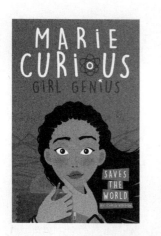

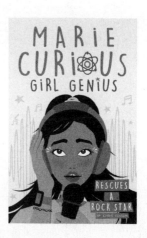

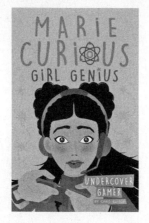